The Golden Age of
Science Fiction

For everyone who understands the true significance of the words 'Klaatu barada nikto'.

The Golden Age of Science Fiction

A Journey into Space with 1950s Radio, TV, Films, Comics and Books

John Wade

PEN & SWORD
HISTORY

First published in Great Britain in 2019 by
Pen & Sword History
An imprint of
Pen & Sword Books Ltd
Yorkshire – Philadelphia

ISBN Hardback 978 1 52672 925 5
ISBN Paperback 978 1 52675 159 1

A CIP catalogue record for this book is
available from the British Library

Typeset in Ehrhardt
by Mac Style

Printed and bound in India by Replika Press Pvt Ltd.

Pen & Sword Books Limited incorporates the imprints of Atlas,
Archaeology, Aviation, Discovery, Family History, Fiction, History,
Maritime, Military, Military Classics, Politics, Select, Transport,
True Crime, Air World, Frontline Publishing, Leo Cooper,
Remember When, Seaforth Publishing, The Praetorian Press,
Wharncliffe Local History, Wharncliffe Transport,
Wharncliffe True Crime and White Owl.

For a complete list of Pen & Sword titles please contact
PEN & SWORD BOOKS LIMITED
47 Church Street, Barnsley, South Yorkshire, S70 2AS, England
E-mail: enquiries@pen-and-sword.co.uk
Website: www.pen-and-sword.co.uk

Or

PEN AND SWORD BOOKS
1950 Lawrence Rd, Havertown, PA 19083, USA
E-mail: Uspen-and-sword@casematepublishers.com
Website: www.penandswordbooks.com

Contents

The kind of alien landscape that, in the 1950s, was amazingly portrayed in science fiction films, painstakingly described in books, cleverly intimated on radio, meticulously illustrated in comics and unconvincingly hammered together in television studios.

Introduction

The 1950s, many aficionados will tell you, was the golden age of science fiction. But how exactly do you define any golden age? Is it an era when a particular art form reached its peak, and was never subsequently bettered? Or is it the time when you personally first discovered, and became overwhelmed by, a specific genre? For me, it was a little of each.

In 1956, when I was at a somewhat tender age, my mother took me to the cinema to see a film called *Ramsbottom Rides Again*, staring Arthur Askey, a popular comedian of the day. On the way, we met a neighbour who asked where we were going. When my mother told her, the neighbour took her aside and explained that she should turn straight round and go home. 'Your son might enjoy the Arthur Askey film, but the second feature will scare the life out of him,' she said. 'He'll have nightmares for weeks.'

My mother was never one to readily take other people's advice, and so we proceeded to the local Odeon.

These were the days when the main film at a cinema was supported by a second feature, sometimes called a B-picture. Usually, these were short films, cheaply made in black and white for the sole purpose of filling out a cinema programme. Sometimes, however, they were films that might have been originally intended as main features, but which didn't quite make the grade. I suspect that the second feature that day, made in garish colour, was one of the latter.

The film had been made in America in 1953, and three years later was doing the rounds of British cinemas as a second feature. It was called *Invaders from Mars*. The majority of films of this type were rated as 'X' certificate, which, in the 1950s, meant no one under the age of sixteen was allowed to see them. For some reason, this one had crept in under the 'A' certificate category, which meant children could watch the film, providing they were accompanied by an adult.

It was the first science fiction film I saw and, far from being scared, I was completely awed by it, partly I suspect because the hero was a boy of about

The Mekon, arch-enemy of Dan Dare, whose comic strip in *Eagle* each week in the 1950s fuelled the fantasies of so many schoolboys of the era.

my own age who discovers, and fights off, a Martian invasion. I wanted to see more, but unfortunately the 'X' certificate system meant I would not be allowed through the doors of any cinema showing similar films for at least another six years. So it was well into the 1960s before I managed to catch up with reruns of 1950s classics like *The Day the Earth Stood Still, Forbidden Planet, This Island Earth* and *Invasion of the Body Snatchers.*

Having discovered science fiction, however, I set out to find other ways to devour it, and soon realised I already had access to one example in *Eagle*, probably the most popular comic among schoolboys of the 1950s where, on the first two pages, Dan Dare fought weekly battles against dastardly aliens

Concept sketch by an *Eagle* studio artist from around 1957, used to reference characters in the *Dan Dare* strip.

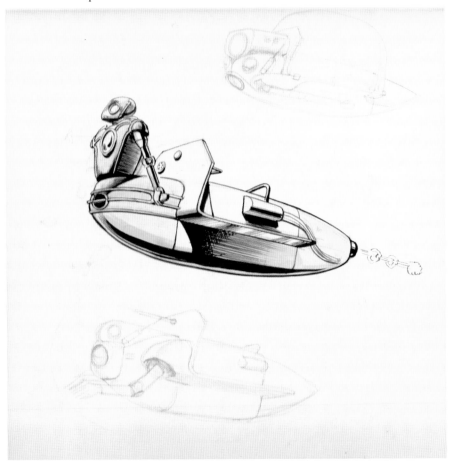

The arrival of *Superman* comics in the UK was a revelation for budding British science fiction addicts.

like The Mekon. I immediately persuaded my parents to cancel my orders for comics like *Beano, Dandy, Topper* and *Beezer* and switch to the mighty *Eagle*. Little could I have envisaged all those years ago that one day, carrying out research for this very book, I would find myself in regular contact with a man called Peter Hampson, the son of Frank Hampson, who created and drew the *Dan Dare* strips; or that I would be privileged to see previously unpublished annotated drawings created by Hampson and his fellow artists as references that ensured the accuracy and continuity of the characters and their surroundings.

I also remembered that I had another example of 1950s science fiction hidden away in my bedroom. It had come courtesy of a fellow pupil in my junior school who had shown me a *Superman* comic, which I managed to prise from his hands by the simple expedient of swapping it for six copies of *Beano*. Having read it from cover to cover, I set about worrying every newsagent in town to find another copy, but I can only assume my school friend had had the comic sent to him by someone in America. English newsagents had never heard of Superman, and it was some years more before the comics arrived in the UK.

Meanwhile, there were other places to find science fiction, among them, surprisingly perhaps, on radio – or the wireless, as we called it then. On *Children's Hour* there were dramatisations of the Angus MacVicar books about Hesikos, the lost planet. And there was the magnificent *Journey Into Space*, of which, a lot more later. On television there was *Quatermass*, which unfortunately for me was deemed unsuitable for children. Not that a little thing like that stood in the way of at least one parent who had allowed me to see *Invaders from Mars* and who permitted me to stay up to see the first instalment – though sadly not subsequent episodes – of *The Quatermass Experiment*. Neither did my parents' broad-mindedness extend to the 1954 television production of *Nineteen Eighty-Four*.

Thankfully, it wasn't long before magazines began to arrive from America with names like *The Magazine of Fantasy and Science Fiction* and *Astounding Science Fiction*, as well as British attempts to emulate them with titles like *Vargo Staten's Science Fiction Magazine*.

Also in Britain at this time, large format science fiction books or omnibuses aimed at a young readership were occasionally published. With a size and shape more usually associated with *Beano, Dandy* and other comic annuals,

The *Quatermass* serials on the somewhat primitive televisions of the 1950s were among the first to be deemed unsuitable for children.

their intermittent arrival would prove to be an exciting source for science fiction and fact, as well as amazingly imaginative artwork that showed how the future might be.

Most of all, however, it was the novels that started to appear from reputable paperback publishers like Penguin, Pan and Corgi that really captured

The first edition of *Vargo Staten's Science Fiction Magazine*, which hit British newsagents in 1954.

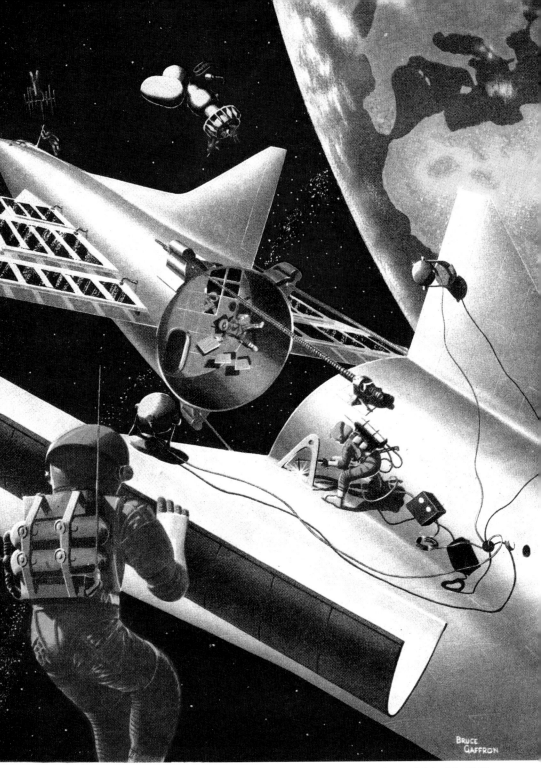

Building a space station: the frontispiece of *Space Story Omnibus*, first published in 1955.

my imagination. If ever proof were needed that the golden age of science fiction had begun, those books upheld that claim. *The Day of the Triffids* was published in 1951 and brought fame to an author with multiple pseudonyms, but who for that book had decided to call himself John Wyndham. The same

Based on descriptions in the book, an artist's impression of what a triffid might have looked like.

year that the triffids first strode across the English countryside, American author Ray Bradbury took us to his own vision of Mars in *The Martian Chronicles*, and two years after that Isaac Asimov's *Foundation* brought us an inter-galactic vision of the future, while Arthur C. Clarke offered his own interpretation of an alien invasion in *Childhood's End*.

In this book I'll tell the story of these and many more aspects of 1950s science fiction. I don't intend to cover every film, book, magazine or television production of the decade, though. This is not, after all, an encyclopaedia of the genre. It's much more a personal account of science fiction in the 1950s as I discovered and revelled in it, sometimes from American imports, but equally from home-grown British writers and productions.

Let others tell you that the golden age of science fiction was the 1930s, when the pulp magazines began; the 1960s, when a 20-year-old Julie Christie riveted the attention of every schoolboy I knew in *A For Andromeda* and the Gerry Anderson puppets thundered onto the small screen; the 1970s and 1980s, in which *Star Wars* reinvented the genre; or even the present day, when so many blockbuster science fiction films are being made in widescreen, with Dolby sound and 3-D.

For me, the super-accuracy and amazing technical quality of today's films, in an age when we are pretty much certain that the rest of our own solar system is likely to be devoid of intelligent life – though who knows what lies in the Universe beyond – pale into insignificance beside stories of people who built rockets in their back gardens and flew them with their nephews and cooks to lost planets, or tales of aliens who wanted to take over, if not our entire world, then at least our bodies.

I grew up in the 1950s, when all this was happening. For me, the decade has to be the true golden age of science fiction.

Chapter One

Science Fiction on Radio

S omeone once said, 'Radio is like television, only the pictures are better.' I first heard the quote from renowned radio producer and writer Charles Chilton, who was prolific within BBC Radio during the 1950s. I met and interviewed him in the early 1980s, and the quotes from him that follow later come from that interview.

Whoever it was that first came up with that quote hit upon one essential aspect of radio drama: the pictures generated in your head when you listen to a radio broadcast are so much more vivid than what is feasible to show on a television screen.

Another radio producer whom I met when I was trying – unsuccessfully as it turned out – to break into writing radio drama, put it this way. 'Let us imagine,' he said, 'that we are adapting the film *Zulu* for radio or television. In the radio version, one of the cast says, "My God, there are thousands of Zulus pouring over that hill, and they're coming straight for us!" Then a suitable sound effect kicks in and the listener sees the scene come horrifyingly to life in his or her head. On television, we would need a cast of thousands to make that same scene work, and the budget isn't going to stand for it. So, instead, we have to make do with seeing a character pointing his head out of a tent and saying to someone inside, "My God, there are thousands of Zulus pouring over that hill, and they're coming straight for us!" What we don't see are the Zulus. That's why "pictures" on the radio are so much better than on television.'

This of course was before the days of computer-generated imagery (CGI), whose advent in the 1970s made the impossible a lot more possible than before. It was certainly true of the 1950s, when science fiction on radio took the listener to the Moon and Mars and many more places beyond. Black and white television dramas of the day with wobbly cardboard scenery could never hope to make those same journeys and destinations seem nearly so realistic.

JOURNEY INTO SPACE

CHARLES CHILTON

UNABRIDGED

To John Wade

A great pleasure to meet you

Charles Chilton

17 Jan 83

PAN BOOKS LTD : LONDON

The title page of *Journey Into Space*, autographed many years ago by Charles Chilton for the author of the book you are now reading.

For many 1950s science fiction fans, radio of the time was where the obsession began.

British radio in the 1950s of course meant, first and foremost, the BBC. Although it was possible to pick up scratchy, fading broadcasts from overseas stations, the mainstay of British radio was the BBC's Light Programme, Home Service and Third Programme. In 1967, Radio 1 was launched to combat the pirate radio stations that had been relaying pop music from ships outside the legal 3-mile broadcasting limit. At the same time, the Light Programme became Radio 2, the Home Service became Radio 4 and the Third Programme became Radio 3. So if radio science fiction was what you craved during that golden age, it was mostly, though not exclusively, to the Light Programme or the Home Service that listeners inevitably turned.

Here are some of the amazing flights of fancy that radio took us on in the 1950s, starting with one of the true greats …

JOURNEY INTO SPACE

On Monday, 21 September 1953, at seven-thirty in the evening, the first episode of a new radio serial was broadcast on the BBC Light Programme. It was like nothing that had been heard on radio before, and its like will probably never be heard again. It was called *Journey Into Space*, with the subtitles *Journey to the Moon* or *Operation Luna*. The *Radio Times*, adding its own subtitle *A Tale of the Future*, had this to say about episode one:

> The year is 1965 and at a proving ground in New Mexico Sir William Morgan, a leading research scientist, is about to launch an experimental space rocket. Meanwhile his son Jet, piloting a super stratoship sixty miles above the Atlantic on its first passenger trip from London to New York, is racing the clock in order to be at his father's side. But at New Mexico there is a hitch which dramatically affects the whole situation …

That brief summation didn't say much about the story that was about to unfold, dealing as it would with a flight to the Moon, encounters with aliens and even a brush with time travel. The difference between the way the series started and the way it developed could well have been down to the rather haphazard way in which it was written.

Don't get the idea from this, however, that the writer was unfit for the job. On the contrary, he was a tremendously successful radio producer whose writing talents kept his listeners on the edges of their seats for weeks, during three series and fifty-eight episodes of *Journey Into Space*. His name was Charles Chilton.

The man behind the series

Charles Chilton was born in North London in 1917. He joined the BBC as a messenger boy at the age of fifteen, later moving up to work in the Corporation's gramophone library. It was here that he discovered a love of jazz and was responsible for the BBC's first jazz programme, *Kings of Jazz*, which he introduced, making him possibly the BBC's first disc jockey. The programme only went ahead, he later explained, when he was able to convince his bosses that jazz music wouldn't contaminate the airwaves.

He was also one of the producers of *The Goon Show* and the *Billy Cotton Band Show*, in which he even managed to introduce a little science fiction to the Sunday lunchtime entertainment with a character in a flying saucer, who was heard to look down on the bandleader from above calling out: 'Hey, you down there with the glasses.' Chilton's versatility led him to producing shows that ranged from comedy classics like *Take It From Here* to documentaries on subjects as diverse as Victorian Britain and the American Civil War.

In the 1960s, Chilton enjoyed tremendous theatrical and film success when his radio programme *The Long, Long Trail* was adapted to become

Charles Chilton, the radio producer and writer behind *Journey Into Space*.

Oh! What a Lovely War, which juxtaposed the horrors of the First World War with music hall songs of the day.

But back in the 1950s, the BBC, with one eye on popular cinema of the day, where films like *Destination Moon* (1950) and *The Day the Earth Stood Still* (1951) were proving popular, identified a need for science fiction on the radio. The problem was they couldn't find anyone to write it. Although essentially a producer, Chilton had already had success in writing fiction for radio in 1949 with *Riders of the Range*, a western series, which also became a comic strip in the *Eagle*. So he stepped forward and offered to try his hand at radio science fiction.

Along with his interest in the American West, Chilton had always loved science fiction, reading magazines like *Amazing Stories* when he was young and devouring the books of H.G. Wells. The influences were later to be seen in his own writing. When, in the first series of *Journey Into Space*, the ship is stuck on the moon, the captain reads to the crew from Wells's *The First Men*

Charles Chilton's comic strip *Riders of the Range*, which was published in the boys' comic *Eagle*.

in the Moon, and when a strange knocking noise is heard from the outside, one of the characters comments: 'It's one of H.G. Wells's lot.'

Although Chilton had no scientific qualifications of his own, he was a keen amateur astronomer and was determined that the science in *Journey Into Space* would be as accurate as possible. So he enlisted Farnborough rocket designer Kenneth Gatland as technical adviser. Under contract as a producer, Chilton didn't get paid for his writing talents. 'In those days the BBC thought that if you were so filled with the urge to write, then they wouldn't stop you,' he commented some years later. 'I think that attitude stopped shortly after the success of *Journey Into Space*.'

Not that the programme was a guaranteed success from the start. After three weeks, the BBC wanted to take it off the air and Chilton was called in by the Head of the Light Programme, who told him he knew it was no good because his grandchildren didn't like it. Chilton persuaded him to let it run for eight weeks, by which time it was so popular that they asked him to keep going. In the end, that first series ran for eighteen episodes.

Chilton wrote the scripts from week to week, not really knowing where it was going next, usually starting the writing on a Friday night, ready for Monday's broadcast. Once, he wrote an episode a week in advance, but when it got to Thursday, he tore it up and started again. He later said that if he had known people were taking it so seriously, he would have been terrified.

Charles Chilton died in 2013, age 95.

Cast and characters

The four main characters of the series were Captain Jet Morgan and his crew of three: Stephen Mitchell, known as Mitch; Doc Matthews; and Lemmy Barnet. During the course of three series there were a few changes of actors.

In series one, Jet Morgan was played by Andrew Faulds and Doc Matthews by Guy Kingsly Poynter. Mitch was played by Bruce Beeby for the first six episodes, and by Don Sharp for the remaining twelve. Lemmy was played by David Kossoff. In series two, Andrew Faulds and Guy Kingsley Poynter played the same characters again, but Mitch was played by Bruce Beeby throughout, and Alfie Bass took over from David Kossoff to play Lemmy halfway through. In series three, Andrew Faulds and Guy Kingsley Poynter

The cast of *Journey Into Space* stand by for take-off around the microphone. Left to right, they are Don Sharp as Stephen Mitchell or Mitch, Andrew Faulds as Jet Morgan, Alfie Bass as Lemmy Barnet and Guy Kingsley Poynter as Doc Matthews.

retained their roles, Alfie Bass played Lemmy and Don Sharp played Mitch throughout.

Andrew Faulds was born in Tanganyika in 1923, the son of missionary parents, and in the years that followed the success of *Journey Into Space*, he had roles in more than twenty-five films, which included *The Trollenberg Terror* (1958), *Blood of the Vampire* (1958), *The Flesh and the Fiends* (1960), *Jason and the Argonauts* (1963) and *Cleopatra* (1963). He subsequently went into politics and became a member of parliament for Smethwick in 1966. He was known for his loud and often controversial opinions and statements in the House. He died in 2000.

Bruce Beeby was an Australian actor, born in 1921, who worked mostly in British films and TV. Among the films he made between 1945 and 1964, he shared credits with Andrew Faulds in *A Matter of WHO*, about the search for a deadly virus. He died in 2013.

Don Sharp was born in Tasmania in 1921. His most famous roles were in horror films for the Hammer Studios, including *The Kiss of the Vampire* (1962) and *Rasputin, the Mad Monk* (1965). In 1965 and 1966, he also directed *The Face of Fu Manchu* and *The Brides of Fu Manchu*. He died in 2011.

Guy Kingsley Poynter was an American actor, born in 1915. His film credits included *Floods of Fear* (1958) and *The Girl Hunters* (1963). He died in 1983.

David Kossoff was a British actor, born in 1919. He left the cast of *Journey Into Space* when he won a part in the film *A Kid For Two Farthings* (1955), and frequently appeared on TV, notably in the sitcom *The Larkins* (1958). He suggested the name Lemuel for the character he originally played in *Journey Into Space*, but Chilton shortened it to Lemmy. He was also well known as a writer and died in 2005.

Alfie Bass was a British cockney actor, born in Bethnal Green, London in 1916. His feature films included *The Lavender Hill Mob* (1951), *Hell Drivers* (1957), *A Tale of Two Cities* (1958) and *Alfie* (1966). He was much loved by the British public for his roles in the TV programmes *The Army Game* (1957–61) and its spin-off, *Bootsie and Snudge* (1960–63).

One other important member of the cast was David Jacobs, whom Chilton had met in Ceylon in 1945 when he worked for a while running radio services for British troops. Before his fame as the host of *Juke Box Jury* and as a radio disc jockey, Jacobs was an impressionist, and played a great many of the ancillary characters in *Journey Into Space*. It was he who, following the roar of a jet engine, announced with a suitable echo effect added to his voice at the start of each week's episode: 'The BBC presents Jet Morgan in … *Journey – Into – Spaaaaace*.'

Music played an integral role in the eerie atmosphere of the programmes. That was down to the talents of composer and conductor Van Phillips. He was a great fan of the theremin, a very early electronic instrument, which consisted of a small box with two antennae protruding from the top. It was played by a musician who never actually touched the instrument. Instead, he waved his hands in close proximity to each of the antennae. One antenna controlled the pitch (high and low notes), and the closer the hand to the antenna, the higher the note. Moving the other hand towards and away from the second antenna increased and decreased the volume. The result was a sound rather like eerie, celestial voices. Van Phillips used it to great

A modern-day version of the theremin, being played by a member of the Swedish music group Detektivbyrån.

success in all three series. In early episodes, the music was pre-recorded and played from acetate discs during the live performances. Later, an eight-piece orchestra played live in the studio.

Van Phillips also put music to a poem called 'The Green Hills of Earth', from a short story in the book of the same name, written by American science fiction author Robert Heinlein. Supposedly sung by conditioned (hypnotised en mass) men from Earth at the end of series three, it was actually performed by the George Mitchell Choir, Mitchell being the man who went on to fame as the creator of *The Black and White Minstrel Show*, a seemingly innocent and immensely popular music show that began in the late 1950s and went on to create controversy in the 1960s for the offence some people took over the way it portrayed blacked-up singers.

The cast of *Journey Into Space* really got into their parts and often visited Chilton, to look with him at the Moon through his telescope, and to imagine where their alter egos were supposed to be. They were also great practical jokers.

Stories were told about David Jacobs pouring a jug of water down Andrew Faulds's trousers while he was at the microphone, live on air. Retaliation came when Jacobs had to use a distorting microphone close to his mouth for a special effect and Faulds smeared it in advance with mustard.

Although *Journey Into Space* was a radio programme, publicity pictures taken of the cast for press releases, pictures in the *Radio Times* and later for book jackets often showed them wearing space suits. They actually only had one suit between them, an experimental one, borrowed from Farnborough's aeronautical research centre, where it was used for atmospheric travel experiments. For the publicity pictures, each of the cast wore the same suit in turn, with a little camera trickery employed to show them all together, suited up, in a single picture. The suit had a helmet, like an upside-down goldfish bowl, but when it was fitted to the suit, it was airtight, so whoever was wearing it had to hold their breath while the cameraman quickly took the picture. If he hadn't moved fast, the actor might have suffocated!

The plots

There were three series of *Journey Into Space* broadcast in the 1950s, each with thirty-minute episodes. Series One, *Operation Luna*, was broadcast from 21 September 1953 to 19 January 1954, the early episodes on Mondays at 7.30 pm and later episodes on Tuesdays at 8.00 pm. There were eighteen episodes. Series Two, *The Red Planet*, was broadcast from 6 September 1954 to 17 January 1955, on Mondays at 7.30 pm and repeated the following Sundays at 6.00 pm. There were twenty episodes. Series Three, *The World in Peril*, was broadcast from 26 September 1955 to 13 February 1956, on Mondays at 7.30 pm and repeated the following Sundays at 6.00 pm. There were twenty episodes.

The stories were told in the style of a diary, kept by Doc Matthews, using his narration to lead into the action, as performed by all the other characters.

Series One, *Operation Luna*, was set in 1965, the year Chilton anticipated men would first walk on the Moon (he was only four years out). The series showed strong signs of the way it had been written, week by week, with twists and turns in the plot and, as Chilton admitted many years later, a great many loose ends that were never tied up.

Although the story was essentially about Rocket Ship *Luna's* voyage to the Moon, it was episode five before the ship actually took off, the first four episodes being concerned with a rocket launched by Jet Morgan's father which crashed on Las Vegas, Jet's meeting with Mitch who invites him to join Operation Luna and a bit of business with suspected spies who never turn up again throughout the series.

On the way to the Moon, radio operator Lemmy hears strange music on his radio. When they land on the Moon, more of Lemmy's strange music is heard, Jet has visions of the past and future, and Doc sees a strange dome over a nearby crater.

As they prepare to leave for home, the ship loses all power and they are stuck on the Moon for a fortnight, during which time they hear strange noises from outside and an unidentified flying object (UFO) lands nearby. When power is mysteriously resumed, they take off, orbit the Moon and encounter a fleet of UFOs that pursues them, accelerating their speed until they pass out.

When they recover, they land on a nearby planet with Earth-like characteristics, which turns out to be the Earth from an earlier period. They have travelled back in time. Another encounter with a UFO takes them to a city of domed buildings, where they speak with a mysterious voice, which, after some discussion, agrees to get them back to the their own time and return them to their spaceship.

The crew takes off and are once again accelerated by the UFOs to time travelling speed. They black out and, when they wake up, they have no memory of what has happened; and cannot understand why their fuel and oxygen levels are much lower than expected, their rations have been replaced with strange food and there is evidence of a pre-historic implement on board that none of them remembers seeing before.

Only Doc's diary, kept throughout the adventure, can tell them what has happened …

Series two, *The Red Planet*, broadcast just under a year after the first series began, was a little more cohesive in the way the plot developed over a series of twenty episodes. It was set in 1971 and, this time, the crew was bound for Mars in the flagship *Discovery*, along with eight other ships and twenty more men.

Central to the plot was a new character, Frank Whitaker, who is on one of the other ships. He behaves oddly, has nightmares along with Lemmy. Eventually the people at Control back on Earth discover that he was born in 1893 and went missing in 1924. After some fun with a meteor shower and what turns out to be fake messages from Earth, Whitaker is injured and dies, at which point his body reverts to being a very old man.

The fleet lands on Mars, there are encounters with what appear to be Earthmen who arrive in a spherical UFO, referred to as a sphere, Jet discovers the ruins of a city that he had dreamt about on his way to Mars, and eventually they meet up with a lot more Earthmen, who have been conditioned in some way to breath the Martian air.

Mitch gets lost in the Martian desert and meets a couple who seem to think they are in Australia, working as sheep farmers. Another conditioned Earthman arrives who thinks he is an Australian flying doctor.

Some members of crew are captured by the Martian Earthmen, and then escape; others get conditioned but manage to pull out of the hypnosis. Eventually the four main characters make it back to their rocket and take off for home, pursued by a fleet of the flying spheres.

Did they make it home? The listening audience had to wait for the next series to find out.

Series three, *The World in Peril*, was broadcast a little over a year after the second series began. This time it's 1972 and the crew of *Discovery* have made it back to Earth, where an astronomer has spotted strange objects far out in space. They turn out to be asteroids that are actually spacecraft carriers. Jet and his crew are sent back to Mars to investigate what seems to be a Martian invasion.

They take off from the Moon, just before the base there is taken over by the approaching Martian invasion fleet. After some problems with strange voices on the trip, they eventually land on Mars, where they end up being captured and held on board one of the asteroids that are ferrying the invasion fleet to Earth. The invasion fleet consists of Earthmen who, over the years, have been abducted and taken to Mars to be conditioned.

After encounters with one of the conditioned Earthmen, they escape and explore the interior of the asteroid. They constantly ignore a mysterious voice telling them to go back. Much to their surprise they then encounter their Lunar Controller, who, it transpires, has been in league with the

Martians. He tells them that when the fleet reaches Earth, everyone there will be conditioned by way of a hypnotic television broadcast. It appears there are no real Martians, only a computerised brain that is giving orders to the conditioned Earthmen.

The crew manages to smash the brain and make their escape, only to find their rocket has been damaged. Using one of the Martian spheres, they transfer to one of their orbiting rockets that had originally accompanied them on the mission and head for Earth. On the way, they send a message to Earth to shut down all television broadcasts. But the Martian fleet overtakes them. Then they crash onto an asteroid, which is the headquarters of the last remaining Martian, a giant whose race is responsible for the giant legends of Earth, from the times when they visited many years before.

Jet and the crew are now prisoners on board the asteroid, part of the invasion fleet. But their message has got though and, on Earth, all television stations are being shut down.

The Martian releases them and gives all conditioned Earthmen the opportunity to return home. Some do, but the majority decide to go on and establish a new civilisation in another solar system.

What came next

Journey Into Space had its critics. Some said that, despite Chilton's determination to keep things as accurate as possible, there were a lot of scientific inaccuracies. One reviewer in the *Radio Times* described it as 'a glorified interstellar horse-opera with no coherent plot, which relied on odd musical arrangements to bolster up the stilted conversations of characters with no substance'.

But the public loved it, and it was praised for being thrilling, fascinating and full of suspense. One episode of *The Red Planet* has gone down in broadcasting history as the last radio show to draw more listeners than the equivalent evening's television programming. Even today it retains its fan base and has initiated many websites.

Seventeen countries bought *Journey Into Space* and it was translated into half a dozen languages, from Romanian to Hindustani. In the mid- to late 1950s, Chilton wrote three novels based on the three series, which were translated into French, Dutch and Italian. He also wrote the stories for comic strips in *Junior Express* comic, the first of which, *Planet of Fear*, was a direct sequel to *World in Peril*. He followed it up by continuing the story with *Shadow Over Britain*, before handing the strip over to another writer at the end of the decade. In 1956, a Chilton-written episode called *Jet Morgan and the Space Pirates* appeared in the *Express Annual* and, the following year, the *Annual* featured another Chiltern story, *Jet Morgan and the Space Castaway*.

Journey Into Space's last outings for radio came in the 1980s and continued on even into the twenty-first century, with three final offerings by Chilton. A 1981 episode of Radio 4's *Saturday Night Theater* featured a one-off radio play called *The Return From Mars*. Another one-hour play called *Frozen in Time* was broadcast in 2008.

They marked the return to radio for the producer/writer who, following the success of the first three series, made a brief move into television, during which time it was suggested that *Journey Into Space* make the transition to TV.

'But I didn't fancy it,' Chilton said many years later. 'In those days, everything on TV was broadcast live in the studio, with cardboard cut-outs for props. I really didn't want to see Jet and the crew on the Moon and then see the background shaking behind them.

The three *Journey Into Space* novels written by Charles Chilton.

'Radio was definitely the best medium for the programme. *Journey Into Space* got into your mind. People believed in it. Many of them thought it was real. You could never achieve that with television back in those days.'

THE LOST PLANET

Poet Henry Wadsworth Longfellow, who was born in 1807 and died in 1882, would seem to have little to do with 1950s science fiction. But he does have a somewhat tenuous connection, because it was he who wrote:

> *Between the dark and the daylight,*
> *When the night is beginning to lower,*
> *Comes a pause in the day's occupations,*
> *That is known as the Children's Hour.*

It was from this verse that the BBC took the name of one of the broadcaster's most popular programmes. *The Children's Hour*, later to drop the definite article and be known simply as *Children's Hour*, was broadcast between 5.00 pm and 6.00 pm every weekday from 1922 to 1961. After that, programmes in the same time slot were broadcast under the title of *For the Young* for three more years. The programme began life on the BBC's regional stations before settling comfortably into its most popular spot on the Home Service.

Children's Hour was a very middle-class kind of programme, which obeyed the BBC's self-imposed rule to inform, educate and entertain. Its magazine-like content ranged from talks such as *The Queens of England*, broadcast in the lead-up to the Coronation of Queen Elizabeth II in 1953, to the jolly japes of *Jennings at School* and, for younger listeners, *Toy Town*. The programme was not averse either to a generous helping of science fiction in the shape of the *Lost Planet* serials.

Written by Angus MacVicar, and based on his own books, the programmes covered interstellar travel as only the 1950s could portray it: a scientist who builds his own spaceship and takes off into the unknown with a motley crew that includes his 16-year-old nephew and his cockney housekeeper.

The man behind the stories

Angus MacVicar was born in 1908, the son of a Church of Scotland Presbyterian minister. As a student, he first studied Arts at Glasgow University, before changing to a Divinity course with thoughts of following in his father's footsteps. A subsequent post as an assistant minister in Glasgow, however, changed his mind and in 1930 he joined the *Campbeltown Courier* local newspaper. It was the start of a life devoted to writing. He published his first novel, *The Purple Rock*, in 1933.

Giving up journalism in favour of becoming a full-time writer, MacVicar became a prolific author, specialising in autobiography, crime thrillers and children's science fiction, the last of which had a certain amount of Christian morality underlying its plots.

His introduction to radio came when the BBC invited him to present an item for *Children's Hour*. The subject was the Scottish herring industry. It was a long way removed from the world of science fiction, but it opened up a new path for him and, over the following years, he wrote more than 500 radio scripts, many of which were adapted from his own books. Among these were the *Lost Planet* series of broadcasts, followed devotedly by children of the 1950s.

MacVicar also developed a relaxed, and easy-to-listen-to microphone technique, which led to him presenting programmes on historical and religious subjects. That in turn led to him becoming a presenter on BBC Television's *Songs of Praise*, a popular programme broadcast from churches around the UK on Sunday evenings.

In 1954, MacVicar wrote a radio series called *The Glens of Glendale*, based on his own experiences as the son of a Scottish minister. The series ran for 100 episodes. In his sixties he wrote a number of gentle and philosophical best-selling novels that, like much of his work, reflected his Christian faith. He died in 2001.

Of all his great many books and radio broadcasts, for the generation of children listening avidly to *Children's Hour* every night in the 1950s, it was his *Lost Planet* science fiction stories that proved to be the most enduring.

The plots

From 1953 to 1960, MacVicar wrote six Lost Planet books: *The Lost Planet, Return to the Lost Planet, Secret of the Lost Planet, Red Fire on the Lost Planet,*

Return to the Lost Planet, one of Angus MacVicar's books that he turned into a radio serial for children.

Peril on the Lost Planet and *Space Agent from the Lost Planet*. It was the first two that won acclaim as radio serials.

To some extent the initial premise of the stories echoed *The First Men in the Moon*, written by H.G. Wells back in 1901, in that it involved the work of a single scientist who financed, built and launched his own rocket ship for the purposes of private space travel. The two men who went to the Moon in Wells's story travelled in a metal and glass sphere, covered with blinds made of a substance that cancelled the effects of gravity. By opening and closing selected blinds, they took off from the Earth and steered their way through space. MacVicar's rocket, however, was powered by something far more reliable: atomic motors.

Exactly how these atomic motors worked was never really explained, because MacVicar's grasp of scientific technology wasn't foremost in the stories. It was the plots, not the science, that held the listeners.

The Lost Planet was the first series to be broadcast. Its title referred to Hesikos, a planet that was said to wander the Universe. It seemed that it had a breathable atmosphere, gravity similar to that of Earth and, what's more, due to the way it wandered the Universe, it would soon be in a position that meant it could be reached by a spaceship, equipped with those aforementioned atomic motors, within a few days.

All this is discovered by 16-year-old Jeremy Grant, who goes to Scotland to stay with his uncle, Dr Lachlan McKinnon, who, it transpires, is building a spaceship to make this very journey.

Uncle Lachlan isn't alone. He has surrounded himself with friends and prospective space travellers that include American engineer Spike Stranahan, another engineer called Kurt Oppenheim, a Swedish professor named Lars Bergman, science student Janet Campbell and, most incongruous of all for a potential astronaut, his housekeeper and cook, Madge Smith.

Unfortunately, Kurt Oppenheim turns out to be a spy, who defects to a rival expedition led by Professor Hermanoff. Now the crew is one light. Who could possibly take the place of Oppenheim? Why, 16-year-old Jeremy, of course. And off they go, in search of Hesikos.

In a few fairly simple plot twists and turns, the spaceship crash-lands on Hesikos, damaging the radio and killing their chances of getting back to Earth. What's more, it seems the planet will be covered in ice and snow come the winter, making it highly unlikely that the crew will survive.

Luckily, Hermnanoff's ship has landed by now and, when the two teams meet up, he agrees to take them back to Earth. But there's a problem: the new ship will now be so overcrowded that they might not be able to take off. Uncle Lachlan decides to sacrifice himself for the good of others (MacVicar's Christian philosophies showing through). He is joined in his exile by his former rival, Professor Hermanoff, and his own engineer, Spike Stranahan.

Safely back on Earth, Morse code messages are received from Hesikos. The trio left behind are alive. A rescue attempt is planned. Which is where the first series finishes.

Return to the Lost Planet showcases MacVicar's Christian attitudes and convictions even more than the first series. For its young listeners, it was also more exciting because it involved actual aliens.

The rescue crew that leaves for Hesikos consists of young Jeremy, Professor Bergman, Janet and Madge. They take off, make the journey through space, land, explore the surface in a jeep that they have brought with them and find the three people that they left behind. It seems they have survived the harsh winter after all. Exploring the planet further, they discover evidence that Hesikos once supported life, but it was destroyed by atomic bombs.

There was clearly an underlying subtext here, which, if not understood by the serial's young listeners, would undoubtedly have been noted by their parents, who at that time were all too aware of the devastating effects of the atomic bombs that were dropped on Hiroshima and Nagasaki towards the end of the Second World War in 1945.

MacVicar's preaching, for want of a better word, continues as the Earthlings discover the people of Hesikos living peacefully deep underground, since their planet's orbit had been destroyed by the atomic bombs. They are humanlike, intelligent and use a machine called an electronome to communicate telepathically.

Their leader is a man called Solveg, who has a daughter called Asa. When the Earth visitors return to the spaceship for the journey home, they take Asa with them. Her aim is to spread the word about the joys of peace and harmony to everyone on Earth.

Angus MacVicar might not have made it as a minister, but he still managed to get his Christian message across, even when writing science fiction for children.

DAN DARE

In an age when the BBC dominated the British airwaves, listening to Radio Luxembourg had a kind of vicarious thrill about it, almost as though the listener was breaking the law. That of course was not the case, since the station, as its name implied, was broadcast, not from a station on British soil, but from what was officially known as the Grand Duchy of Luxembourg.

The station began in 1924 when two brothers, François and Marcel Anen, enthralled by the prospect of radio communication, installed a transmitter in the attic of their house in Luxembourg City. In the years that followed, they set about broadcasting music and sports reports, gradually increasing the power of their transmitters. The station was initially multilingual, but

Radio Luxembourg exhibiting in 1958 at Expo 58, also known as the Brussels World's Fair, the first major World's Fair after the Second World War.

in 1933, an English language service began. By the 1950s, it was possible to pick up Radio Luxembourg in the UK, albeit only on long wave and with a weak signal that continually faded in and out.

It became known as *The Station of the Stars* and was the illicit joy of many a schoolboy and schoolgirl, listening, under their bedcovers at night, to one of the few sources of pop music available to them on the radio.

From July 1951 to May 1956, at 7.15 pm each week night, Radio Luxembourg broadcast *The Adventures of Dan Dare*. The hero was a space explorer who came up against, and battled, numerous aliens. His beginnings in the *Eagle* comic and subsequent exploits will be discussed later. Meanwhile, here's how his adventures came to be on Radio Luxembourg.

One thing that was alien to the ears of regular BBC listeners was hearing advertisements on their radios. They were there in abundance on Radio Luxembourg, and certain programmes were financially sponsored by advertisers. *The Adventures of Dan Dare* was sponsored by Horlicks, a nutritional malt milk drink, traditionally drunk warm at night before bedtime.

Although broadcast from Luxembourg, *Dan Dare* was very much an English production. It was produced at a studio in London by John Glyn-Jones, who later won fame as a British television and film actor. Each episode was recorded onto wax discs, which were shipped to Luxembourg for transmission back to Britain.

The voice that announced the start of each episode would have been familiar to many a UK listener. He was Bob Danvers-Walker, a radio and newsreel announcer, best known as the voice behind *Pathé News*, which was shown in British cinemas. Dan Dare was played by Noel Johnson, who had already won fame on British radio as Dick Barton, Special Agent, a kind of early James Bond whose adventures had already been heard on the BBC Light Programme from 1946 until 1951.

With the sponsorship of Horlicks behind the *Dan Dare* programmes, young listeners were invited to join the Horlicks Spaceman's Club. This was likely to have been in reaction to the Ovaltineys Club developed in the 1930s for young people by Horlicks's main rival, Ovaltine. Members of the Horlicks Spaceman's Club could, for the price of a few pennies and a label from a Horlicks jar, buy a Spaceman's Club Handbook that offered details about Dan Dare and his friends, how his Spacefleet was formed, their ships

The legend of Dan Dare lives on long after the Radio Luxembourg broadcasts have been forgotten. This is a display case at the Atkinson Museum in Southport, where Dan Dare's creator Frank Hampson grew up.

and equipment. Also on offer were a Dan Dare Tie, Spacefleet Service Identity Card, Spaceman's Club Badge, Dan Dare Spaceship Cup and a Dan Dare Periscope.

The *Dan Dare* production didn't begin and end with Radio Luxembourg. The show was also broadcast in Australia, and the scripts were translated into Spanish to be acted by Spanish actors for a radio series in Spain.

The Horlicks Spaceman's Club Handbook and badge, issued to the young listeners of *Dan Dare* on Radio Luxembourg.

OTHER RADIO PRESENTATIONS

In the days before television was the major source of evening entertainment, families would huddle around the radio and listen to plays, of which there were several broadcast every week.

In 1950, the BBC broadcast a radio adaptation of H.G. Wells's *The War of the Worlds*. This story had already won a certain amount of notoriety in America, due to a radio broadcast in 1938 by actor, director, writer and producer Orson Welles. The urban myth is that this broadcast caused nationwide panic as Americans fled from their radios and took to the streets under the mistaken impression that a Martian invasion was actually happening. The truth is less dramatic. Although there is some evidence that the play disturbed a few, it's unlikely that it caused the widespread pandemonium that the myth perpetuates. It's also unlikely that British radio listeners reacted in a similar way when they heard their own adaptation on BBC radio.

In 1951, an adaptation of Paul Capon's book *The Other Side of the Sun*, published the previous year, was broadcast. Capon, who later went on to be Head of the Film Department at Independent Television News, began writing science fiction in the early 1950s. He specialised in time travel, alien invasions and lost civilisations. *The Other Side of the Sun* was the first of three books about the discovery of an Earthlike planet usually invisible because it was hidden from human eyes behind the sun. The other two books in Capon's trilogy were *The Other Half of the Planet*, published in 1952, and *Down To Earth*, in 1954.

The prime slot for BBC radio drama was held by *Saturday Night Theatre*, which ran ninety-minute plays every Saturday night from 1943 until 1997. The plays were solidly grounded in their entertainment values. Some were originals, written especially for *Saturday Night Theatre*, others were based on book adaptations; some of these were science fiction stories.

Writers whose work was adapted for *Saturday Night Theatre* in the 1950s included American author Ray Bradbury and English authors Arthur C. Clarke and John Wyndham, each of whose work will be discussed in more depth later.

MEANWHILE IN AMERICA

Television came to American households earlier than in Britain. As it took a hold, American radio drifted away from drama and more towards music and news programmes. So by the start of the 1950s, American radio had already broadcast most of its better-known science fiction dramas. *Buck Rogers* and *Flash Gordon* had both come and gone by 1950. *Superman*, however, which began serialisation in 1940, endured until 1952.

It's hard to imagine how plots that relied on a flying man performing amazing feats of superhuman proportions could really come across on radio, for which reason most of the storylines were more like mystery detective stories. The science fiction element was allowed to creep in when stories dealt with the hero's extraterrestrial origins or when he was fighting the effects of kryptonite, a deadly substance that could sap his powers and eventually destroy him.

From 1950 to 1955, the American ABC network broadcast *Space Patrol*, which started as a television serial before transferring to radio. It concerned the adventures of Commander Buzz Corry. Listeners to the radio show, as well as viewers of the television version, were invited to join a fan club that would make them space cadets and, more importantly to the sponsors, buy cosmic smoke guns and other such like space paraphernalia. The stories were scientifically plausible for their time.

Ken Meyer and Ed Kemmer in the American television series *Space Patrol*.

Another American television/radio collaboration was *Space Cadet*. Its hero, Tom Corbett, was a teenager who was a cadet in the Solar Guards, a kind of interplanetary police force. Its influence was a 1948 novel called *Space Cadet* by renowned science fiction writer Robert Heinlein. His hero had a different name, Matt Dodson, but his job of helping to preserve peace in the Solar System, was much the same.

'Who knows what evil lurks in the hearts of men? The Shadow knows!' Those were opening lines of *The Shadow* series that started in 1937 and continued over 600 episodes until 1954. The hero had superhuman powers and many of the stories involved traditional science fiction themes.

Fantasy and science fiction featured in many of the plot lines of *The Mysterious Traveller*, which started on radio in 1943 and continued until 1952. It was primarily a crime series, but individual episodes covered plots that involved robots, telepathy, time travel and a crashed Martian spaceship.

Much of American radio science fiction was aimed at children. But from 1950 to 1952, the Mutual Broadcasting System offered possibly as many as 100 thirty-minute episodes of a show called *2000 Plus*, which appealed more to adults. All its stories were originals, written for the series. Titles, which sum up the content pretty well, included *Men From Mars*, *Space Wreck*, *The Flying Saucers*, *The Insect*, *When the Machines Went Wild*, *When the Worlds Met* and *Worlds Apart*.

At the same time, *Dimension X* and *X Minus One*, broadcast on NBC from 1950 to 1958, featured adaptations of well-known science fiction books, including stories from Ray Bradbury's *The Martian Chronicles* collection and Robert Heinlein's short story *Requiem*.

Science fiction magazines of the time also inspired American radio programmes. *Tales of Tomorrow*, in 1953, was sponsored by the magazine *Galaxy* and comprised adaptations of stories from that magazine. *Exploring Tomorrow*, from 1957 until 1958, took stories from *Astounding* magazine. Short stories from both contemporary and classical authors were also adapted for the radio anthology series *Sleep No More*, from 1956 to 1957.

Radio science fiction in America began a few decades before the start of the 1950s, and continued well into the 1960s. Although some of the better-known science fiction heroes had disappeared by the start of the decade, that golden age from 1950 to 1959 still saw the best of the rest before the genre inevitably made the move to television.

Advertisements from the 1950s show how television was both a novelty and a luxury for most people.

Chapter Two

Science Fiction on Television

At the start of the 1950s, very few families in Britain owned a television, and the few that did had only one channel to watch. It came, of course, from the BBC. The event that, more than any other, encouraged people go out and buy televisions was the Coronation of Queen Elizabeth II on 2 June 1953. After that, televisions gradually began to become part of the furniture. By the end of the decade, most homes had a television in the corner of the lounge, and the number of channels available had risen to two. The second channel was ITV, which began broadcasting in September 1955, and required existing televisions to be converted with a special box on the back.

Both channels broadcast programmes only in black and white. Regular colour broadcasts didn't begin until 1967, and needed new televisions to receive the programmes. Most viewers stuck to their old televisions and viewed the colour programmes in black and white.

Watching television in the early 1950s was something that had to be learned, according to the *1954 Television Annual*, which had a whole chapter devoted to what it called *Fallacies and Facts for Beginner Viewers.*

One fallacy it was keen to dispel was the necessity to watch TV in the dark. Early televisions, whose small screens were green when turned off, lost contrast in the picture if a room light was turned on. But by 1954, new screen technology meant that viewing with a table lamp situated behind the set was recommended by the *Annual*, which added, with a nice touch of political incorrectness, 'allowing mother to get on with darning the socks if she wants to'.

Neither was it desirable to have a big screen, the *Annual* assured its readers. Purchasers of moderate priced televisions were told to feel in no way inferior to those who lavished money on larger screens. The truth was that most drawing rooms needed no more than a 12-inch screen. Anything more than that would reveal the dark lines that made up the picture, meaning viewers would have to sit a long way from the set in order to appreciate what they were watching. In many homes, it was rather condescendingly suggested, that would mean sitting in the hall.

If watching television of the 1950s was fraught with such complications, they were nothing compared to the difficulties and stress of making the programmes and broadcasting them live – and science fiction shows, with their so often necessary special effects, must have been the most stressful of all.

Nigel Kneale was the television and film writer behind *Quatermass*, the hero of BBC Television's first science fiction serial, which began broadcasting in July 1953. I met and interviewed Kneale many years later towards the end of his long and illustrious career in film and TV scriptwriting, and he told me a story that typified the angst of broadcasting science fiction in those days.

'In 1955, we were broadcasting a play called *The Creature*,' he explained. 'It was about the Abominable Snowman. The production was live, and actors were in a studio surrounded by scenery meant to look like an ice cave in the Himalayas. About fifteen minutes before the end of the play, the actors, wrapped in the kind of clothes needed when you're supposed to be 20,000 feet up a mountain, looked out of the cave and there, in plain view, was a man in shirtsleeves, sweeping up the snow. It turned out he was a cleaner who wanted to get home early and so had started clearing up the set while the live broadcast was still going on.'

During the 1950s, Kneale was a stalwart of British TV science fiction writing, with his name credited on some of the broadcaster's most important and memorable productions. In those days the live broadcasts were made from Alexandra Palace, which still stands at the top of a hill in North London.

'At the end of an evening of broadcasting, I used to walk out onto the top of the hill and look down at all the houses below us with television aerials on their roofs, and I'd think to myself how strange it was that people in all those houses have been watching what we have just been doing in that building behind me,' he said. 'It was exhilarating in a way that programme makers today could never feel.'

My abiding memory of Kneale is when he asked me if I'd like to see the monster from *The Quatermass Experiment*. This was the first of three *Quatermass* serials in which a huge man-turned-into-a-plant monster oozes

How the Alexandra Palace looked in 1952. The BBC's aerial mast used to broadcast television in the 1950s can be seen emerging from behind the building.

down the walls of Westminster Abbey. Naturally I said yes, and Kneale went to a box in the corner of the room, from which he produced an old pair of industrial gloves, covered in pieces of leather, twigs, small branches, dead leaves and various other bits of garden debris. Placing his fingers in the gloves, he wiggled them about in front of his face.

'Pretty scary, eh?' he said. Well, maybe not for me there in the front room of his South London home, but for a whole generation of television science fiction watchers thirty years before, it was a different matter entirely.

Nigel Kneale's name crops up in connection with several TV science fiction programmes discussed here. All his quotes, and many of the facts about BBC productions, come from the interview I carried out with him in the 1980s. He died in October 2006

QUATERMASS

For a generation of television science fiction viewers, the very name Quatermass conjured up visions of monsters and mayhem. Yet there was nothing intrinsically evil about Professor Bernard Quatermass himself. He was simply an eminent professor who got caught up in horrific situations.

Quatermass had three outings on British television in the 1950s and a later one in the 1970s. It was the three initial serials, however, that were the groundbreakers, each better than the previous one, and each guaranteed to scare the life out of its viewers.

The man behind Quatermass

Nigel Kneale, the quietly spoken, gentle man who scared television viewers so much in the 1950s and who, more than anyone, was responsible for the

Nigel Kneale demonstrates his home-made monster that scared television viewers in the first *Quatermass* series.

BBC adopting the *Not Suitable For Children* slogan that prefaced certain programmes, was born in 1922 at Barrow-in-Furness in the north of England. At the age of six he was taken to the Isle of Man, where his father was a newspaper owner and editor. When he left school, Kneale could have been a journalist, but decided that the kind of stories he most liked were the ones he made up in his head. He studied law for a while but didn't enjoy it and returned to England to earn his living.

He did some acting and wrote a good many short stories. In 1950, his short story anthology, *Tomato Caine and Other Stories*, won the Somerset Maugham Award, a literary prize made each year. It brought prestige, but no great commercial success.

His love of storytelling, however, brought him to BBC radio with his own unique brand of plays, including one that involved a haunted telephone line, which relied strongly on the use of sound effects – the way radio drama should be, in his opinion. From there, he worked his way into BBC Television, where he was initially involved in a soon-to-be-forgotten children's puppet show.

'Back in those days, very little drama was written for television,' he said later. 'I was one of just two staff writers servicing the whole drama department with adaptations from radio, or of stage plays and books. When I had been there about a year, there suddenly came a demand to fill a slot, and so I wrote *The Quatermass Experiment*. It was the first adult science fiction drama written for television and entirely my own conception.'

Part of that conception was, of course, the wonderful name of Kneale's hero, and it is tempting to wonder if the serials would have been quite so emotive if the principal character had been called Professor John Smith. So where did the writer find such a memorable name?

'The London phone book,' he said. 'On the Isle of Man where I grew up there were a lot of names beginning with "Q", which was what started me thinking. I found four Quatermasses in the phone book and none of them looked particularly troublesome – no Quatermass QC or anything like that. After the first series was televised I heard from several Quatermasses. They were market traders in London's East End. One said his customers had started calling him professor.'

As well as his television work, Kneale also wrote film scripts, notably adaptations of John Osborne's *Look Back in Anger* and *The Entertainer* in 1958 and 1960. He also wrote for Hammer Films.

Nigel Kneale was best known, however, as the man who, in the words of one critic, was a 'master of the narrative twist which plunges you deeper into a swamp of fear'.

The Quatermass Experiment

On 18 July 1953, to the sound of *Mars* from Gustav Holst's *Planet Suite*, episode one of the first *Quatermass* serial lit up the small-screened televisions of the UK. An estimated 3.4 million people watched it and, by the end of the six-part serial, that audience had risen to more like 5 million, which must surely have represented a major proportion of television owners in Britain at that time. Professor Quatermass was played by Reginald Tate, a popular film and television actor of the day.

As the first episode opens, Professor Quatermass of the British Experimental Rocket Group is anxiously awaiting the return of the first

Duncan Lamont as Victor Carroon emerges from the spaceship with the aid of Reginald Tate as Professor Bernard Quatermass and Isabel Dean as Judith Carroon in episode one of *The Quatermass Experiment*.

manned spaceflight. It crashes on a house in Wimbledon in South London. When Quatermass arrives at the crash site he discovers a peculiar anomaly: three men went into space in the rocket, but only one has returned, even though the suits of the other crew members are still intact and instruments indicate that the rocket's doors have never been opened. The single survivor's name is Victor Carroon and he is badly injured.

Before Carroon can get well, however, he is abducted by foreign agents, but that's just the start of his problems. It seems he has absorbed the consciousness of his two crewmates and, to make matters worse, there is a peculiar alien life form growing on his arm.

Over the course of six episodes, the alien organism takes over more and more of Carroon's body, until he is completely transformed into a huge plantlike monster. Chasing the rapidly mutating Carroon across London, Quatermass, his companions and the British police eventually succeed in tracking him/it down to Westminster Abbey, where the monster is seen slithering down a wall close to Poet's Corner.

Quatermass realises that if the plant thing that was once Victor Carroon is capable of sporing and reproducing at such a fast rate, it means it could soon take over all humanity and bring about the end of life on Earth. How can he possible destroy it? By giving it a good talking to, of course.

Approaching the monster in the Abbey, Quatermass appeals to what remains of the humanity of the three rocket crew members whose consciousness is buried deep in the monster. As a result the monster turns against itself and dies.

'I never really saw it as science fiction,' Kneale revealed some years later. 'It was more of a send-up of the genre. In fact, I lampooned science fiction films of the day as part of the plot set in a cinema where a film called *Planet of the Dragons* is on the screen.'

As Carroon became more and more engulfed by the monster, it became completely unnecessary to have an actor in the part at all. Instead, truckloads of leaves and branches were brought into the studio and people buried themselves in the debris, moving it around in what was hoped looked an ominous way. Duncan Lamont, who had played Victor Carroon before he totally metamorphosed into the monster, felt he had a duty to be among those who helped with the effects.

The way live television was put together in the 1950s is exemplified by the fact that, as the first episode of *The Quatermass Experiment* was broadcast, Kneale had only written four episodes and was just starting on the fifth. They were already committed to finishing the serial when he revealed to his BBC bosses that he wanted to use Westminster Abbey for the final episode. It caused some consternation.

Kneale wanted to use the location because the final episode was due to be broadcast not long after the Queen's Coronation in June 1953, and Westminster Abbey was still fresh in the minds of viewers. It soon became clear, however, that the authorities were not going to let the television crews anywhere near the interior of the Abbey.

The solution was to find a picture of Poet's Corner in an old guide book, blow it up, make a hole in it and for Kneale to stick his home-made monster gloves through it while wiggling his fingers a lot.

The success of *The Quatermass Experiment* wasn't immediate. The BBC viewed the programme with a certain amount of discomfort, wondering what kind of trouble it might cause. The critics had little enthusiasm, pointing out how unrealistic it was. But the public watched it in horrified fascination and loved it.

When the film rights were sold, Kneale was not booked to write the screenplay. Instead, an American writer and star were brought in to ensure its success in America.

Kneale had to content himself with the fee he had received from the BBC for the six-part TV serial. He was paid about £125.

Quatermass II

On 22 October 1955, the strains of Holst's *Mars* from *The Planet Suite* once again heralded the arrival of Nigel Kneale's hero on the small screen for the first episode of *Quatermass II*. This time the leading part was taken by English theatrical actor John Robinson, necessitated by the untimely death of Reginald Tate only a month before filming began on the second serial.

The month before, ITV had been launched as the BBC's first rival television channel. With the success of *The Quatermass Experiment* a few years before, the new serial was commissioned in an attempt to combat the opposition and retain viewers.

The plot and the production were both more ambitious than the first serial. At the start, Professor Quatermass is recovering from news that his plans to build a base on the Moon have been put on hold following the explosion of one of his nuclear test rockets in Australia, killing hundreds of staff.

Back in England he sets off to investigate a fall of meteorites. When a colleague investigates further, one of the meteorites sprays him with ammonia and a strange mark appears on his face. Coincident with this, Quatermass discovers that a nearby village has been demolished and a huge, heavily armed industrial plant is being built on the site. It seems to bear an uncanny resemblance to Quatermass's proposed Moonbase.

Over the course of six episodes, a few things come to light. The meteorites are being launched from an orbiting asteroid. The industrial plant is full of pipelines and huge domes full of poisonous gas and a strange slime, which, on analysis, proves fatal to mankind. More and more people end up with the strange marks on their faces, pretty much indicative that their minds have been taken over.

It turns out of course that what is actually happening is that Earth is under attack from aliens who breathe ammonia and who travel to Earth in the meteorites. Here they have the ability to take over human minds, notably a good proportion of the British Government, before being transported into tanks of slime where they can grow into monsters ready to destroy everyone on Earth.

Luckily, our hero has a spare nuclear rocket, called *Quatermass II*. He flies it to the asteroid and, after some shenanigans with one of his team who accompanies him and turns out to be a traitor, he uses the rocket's motor to blow up the asteroid. Whereupon everyone on Earth who had been marked and had their minds taken over is freed.

Thanks to a bigger budget than that of the first serial, much of the action in *Quatermass II* could be pre-filmed for insertion into the live broadcasts. The base built by the aliens was a particularly impressive location. It was actually the Shell Haven Oil Refinery in Essex, a place full of towers, pipes and domes.

'The great thing about an oil refinery is that there are few people on site,' said Kneale, speaking about the production later. 'We were warned not to smoke, but apart from that we were left very much to ourselves. When I first visited the location, I had a rough story in mind, but no script. The location and its potential had a huge influence on the way the story developed.'

Huge spherical containers at the futuristic-looking Shell Haven oil Refinery, where the second *Quatermass* series was filmed.

Despite the success of his first *Quatermass* serial, *Quatermass II* still had an uphill battle for acceptance among the BBC hierarchy. Kneale received a memo from the Head of Drama saying he didn't like any of it. Kneale wrote back to say that the film rights had sold based on the first episode alone, and that the *Daily Mail* and *Daily Express* were in a bidding war to run the story as a serial. And, of course, as before, the public loved every minute of it.

The six episodes went out on Saturday nights, when they were telerecorded on 35mm film and repeated on Monday nights. This meant that some of the content could be reperformed if it didn't go quite right first time around, so that the repeat was better than the first broadcast. Before that, most repeats meant that the entire production was acted live the second time as well as the first. *Quatermass II* was one of the first BBC dramas to be telerecorded and rebroadcast in this way.

Quatermass and the Pit

On 22 December 1958, to the music this time of Trevor Duncan, the pseudonym of radio producer Leonard Trebilco, *Quatermass and the Pit*, the third serial, began a six-week run on BBC television. This time the part of the professor was played by theatre, film and television actor André Morell.

During excavation work for a new building in London, workmen discover strange artefacts. The fictional street is identified in the opening scene with two signs: a modern one calling it Hobbs Lane, and an older one beneath referring to it as Hob's Lane. The significance of that becomes apparent later.

First the workmen find a strange skull, then a buried spaceship is gradually revealed the deeper the workmen dig. An army colonel called in claims it is an unexploded German bomb, left over from the Second World War. Quatermass thinks different. It transpires that, over many years, there has been a lot of poltergeist activity and sightings of ghosts in the area around Hobbs Lane. Hob is an ancient word for the Devil.

André Morell (left) as Professor Bernard Quatermass and Cec Linder as Dr Matthew Roney, watched over by one of the creatures from the space capsule in a scene from *Quatermass and the Pit*.

It takes six episodes to discover that the spaceship is 5 million years old and came from Mars when the planet was inhabited. It seems the Martians visited earth in ancient times when primitive men were taken back to Mars, genetically altered to give them telepathy and telekinesis powers and then returned to Earth. With Mars dying, the Martians' plan was to change ancient man's minds and abilities to match their own and then inhabit the Earth. Unfortunately the Martian race wiped itself out before the plan was completed and the spaceship discovered in Hobbs Lane was one that crash-landed on Earth at some point.

The problem is that it is now coming back to life. It's not, as the army colonel maintains, a Nazi propaganda weapon, but a real-life Martian spaceship. Most people who come near are attacked with a kind of mass psychosis that begins driving those affected to start attacking one another in the way the Martians did all those millions of years before.

In a plot that is a clever combination of science fiction and the paranormal, the climax in the last episode sees a huge apparition of the Devil rise up and float over London. Luckily, Quatermass remembers the legends that demons are allergic to iron and water. With the help of a fellow scientist, who takes over after Quatermass succumbs to psychic pressure, an iron chain, grounded in wet earth, is hurled into the apparition.

The Devil dissolves, the spaceship crumbles, those who have survived get their minds back and the terrified television viewing audience is left in shock at the realisation that mankind is descended from Martians.

As with the other two *Quatermass* serials, the third one was also broadcast live, but with between a quarter and half of every episode pre-filmed for insertion into the live broadcasts. These were mostly places where some of the more ambitious special effects were required.

'We filmed it at studios in Hammersmith,' Kneale recalled some years later. 'We filled the studio floor with mud and gradually spread it further and further up the walls to give the impression of digging deeper and deeper. The Martian spaceship was made of fibreglass. It was probably the biggest and most expensive prop the BBC had ever built for a television serial until then.'

The third serial was the best, attracting 11 million viewers for the last episode. It was also given the biggest budget and was a success from the word go. Hammer Films bought the rights, turning the story into a

Three books of the *Quatermass* scripts, published by Penguin in 1959 and 1960.

successful colour film in 1967, which shifted the action to the building of a new underground train line. Nigel Kneale wrote the screenplay.

André Morell had first been offered the part of Professor Quatermass for *The Quatermass Experiment*, but at the time there was no script, only an idea. Kneale described it to the actor, who turned it down because he said he couldn't risk his career on it. For *Quatermass and the Pit*, he was approached again, stepped into the role and became, what most agree, the best Quatermass ever.

Scripts for the first three *Quatermass* serials were published by Penguin in 1959 and 1960.

Quatermass postscripts

In 1979, more than twenty years after the third serial on BBC Television, Nigel Kneale revisited his most popular character. The plot was an interesting one, with Quatermass as an old man battling strange goings on among young people and hippies calling themselves Planet People who were being willingly abducted by a strange force, believing they were being transported to a new life on a new planet. The plot involved current trends and an open-ended story rather than the kind of mystery that was neatly tied up at the end of each of the previous three serials. The BBC lost faith in the idea and it was taken over by ITV, but Kneale wasn't happy with the way it all came together.

'The demand from the film company was to make a four-part television serial which could also become a ninety-minute film,' he said later. 'That was a bad commercial idea. The serial would be too long and the film too short. So I ended up writing something in the middle that could be lengthened or shortened. That's a salesman's idea, not a creative idea.'

To make matters worse, Kneale's previous project had been a one-off television play called *The Stone Tape*, a kind of science fiction ghost story, which involved the stone of an old building acting as a recording medium for past events, inevitably releasing an evil force. Those who remember *The Stone Tape* – and few do – recall it as one of the most terrifying plays seen on television.

'The production took place during a time of industrial action,' said Kneale. 'We just about managed to get it finished in time to go out at Christmas, and there was no press showing. I got no reaction from anyone at the BBC or any of the critics. I thought I had created something terrible that no one would talk about. It was in that state of mind that I started writing the fourth *Quatermass* script. It was no way to go into a project of that size.'

Two other more amusing postscripts

The week following the final episode of *Quatermass and the Pit*, in an episode of *Hancock's Half Hour*, popular comedian of the day Tony Hancock discovers a strange object in his back garden. Everyone tells him it is an unexploded German bomb. He, however, maintains that it's a Martian spaceship. 'Look, it's got *Achtung* written on the side,' he says. 'That's Martian for Acton.'

In 1959, *The Goon Show*, on BBC Radio, broadcast an episode called *The Scarlet Capsule*, which also parodied *Quatermass and the Pit*. It was something that the show had done before. Previously they had parodied another Nigel Kneale script for George Orwell's novel *Nineteen Eighty-Four*. In the *Goon Show* version, Spike Milligan, star and writer of the show, was heard wandering around, reciting, 'It's great to be alive in 1985.'

Which brings us to …

NINETEEN EIGHTY-FOUR

In 1948, George Orwell completed a dystopian novel that concerned a frightening future where everyone's actions are monitored and controlled by Big Brother. The novel, which was published in 1949, was called *Nineteen Eighty-Four*, the year in which the story was set. Today, the novel has become a classic, with the words 'Big Brother' entering the English language to describe a person or organisation that sets out to exert complete control over the lives of all. But in the 1950s, when the BBC first thought of adapting it as a television play, the book was little known.

Briefly, the story concerns its hero, Winston Smith, who works in the Ministry of Truth, where he rewrites documents and adjusts photographs to conform with the continually changing versions of history circulated by the State. Winston rebels, he meets fellow rebel Julia, they indulge in a forbidden romance and are eventually caught by the Thought Police. Interrogated by a man who he thought was on his side, Winston is slowly educated – another way of saying mentally tortured – until eventually he is taken to the fabled Room 101, where those who enter are forced to face their own greatest fears. In Winston's case, that means a cage of rats. He breaks down under the torture and betrays Julia but eventually learns to love Big Brother, just like everybody else.

Summing up *Nineteen Eighty-Four* in this somewhat simplistic way does not come close to doing justice to this remarkable book. But hopefully it's enough to illustrate that it was not the kind of thing the BBC would normally think about broadcasting live on a Sunday evening. The corporation's *Sunday Night Theatre* series, which ran from 1950 to 1959, was more likely to show original British plays, a few adaptations of the likes of George Bernard Shaw or Shakespeare, with an occasional foray into American classics. A play about a future version of Britain, renamed Airstrip One and under State control, a lying government spying on its citizens, illicit love affairs, torture and defeat of the main character was the last thing that Sunday night viewers, the majority of whom would never have heard of Orwell's book, expected to see on the small black and white screens in the corners of their lounges on their return from church.

One of the people who pressed for the BBC to adapt Orwell's book for the small screen was Kenneth Tynan, a renowned theatre critic who, in the 1950s, worked on the *Evening News* and *Guardian* and was also involved with the BBC Script Unit. The idea was supported by the BBC's Assistant Controller of Television, Cecil Madden, who suggested the idea to Rudolph Cartier, who had worked as producer on *The Quatermass Experiment*. The idea was kicked around for a while, with most agreeing that it could not be adapted for mainstream television, until it landed on the desk of BBC Script Unit stalwart Nigel Kneale, who decided to have a go at it.

Nineteen Eighty-Four was broadcast on Sunday, 12 December 1954. Winston Smith was played by English actor Peter Cushing, best known for sinister performances in Hammer horror films, including his appearance as Victor Frankenstein, he of monster-making fame. André Morell, later to find fame as the third Quatermass, played O'Brien, the man Winston thought to be his friend, but who turns out to be his torturer. Donald Pleasence, another English actor who specialised in evil characters, played Syme, a colleague of Winston's whose work involves removing certain words from the English language so that it becomes impossible for people to discuss or even think about concepts the government deems unsuitable.

'Visually, the production was livelier than most of the stuff that went out at that time,' said Nigel Kneale, speaking about the production some years later. The live performance was also not without its difficulties and stress-inducing moments, as Kneale also recalled.

'A key element in the plot revolved around a paperweight, found by the hero in an antique shop, and we had a Victorian example to be used in the play. It was left on the prop table, and ten minutes before we went out live, someone stole it. The producer said he was going to black out the studio so that the culprit could return the crucial prop and no questions would be asked. The lights went out. The lights came back on. The prop was still missing. The live performance began, in the knowledge that the paperweight would be needed about halfway through the play. So the stage manager's assistant went home on a bus, borrowed his sister's toy Mickey Mouse snow dome, took a bus back to the studio and got it onto the set in the nick of time.'

The production budget was initially set at £3,000, which was extremely high for the day, and rose even more when Cartier asked for extra funding to have music written specially for the presentation. As a result, music was written by composer John Hodgkis, who conducted an orchestra playing live during the performance from a separate studio.

The budget also had to support twenty-eight different sets and six film sequences, inserted between the live action to give actors, crew and cameras time to move from set to set.

In writing the small screen adaptation, Kneale had given consideration to changing the gloomy ending of the book into something a little more positive, but in the end decided that to do so would be to do what Winston Smith was forced to do to so-called history in his job at the Ministry of Truth. So the downbeat ending stayed.

The BBC, cast, crew and writer had expected some kind of public backlash against the production, but weren't prepared for just how severe it would be.

'As I left the studio after the broadcast, I casually asked our receptionist if there had been any reaction,' said Kneale. 'I was told that complaints were already pouring in from viewers who objected to seeing scenes of torture on their televisions. Peter Cushing suffered more than most because his name was in the phone book, and he got streams of complaining telephone calls. He had to take a holiday.'

The play, originally broadcast on a Sunday evening, was due to be repeated the following Thursday. The BBC soon began to have doubts as to the wisdom of a repeat. The press coverage was remarkable as almost all the papers denounced the production with headlines crying *This Play Must Not Go Out Again.* There were even questions in Parliament when five Conservative MPs tabled a motion deploring 'the tendency, evident in recent BBC television programmes, notably on Sunday evenings, to pander to sexual and sadistic tastes'.

In the few days between the initial Sunday night performance and the Thursday repeat, the BBC hastily called together a chat programme to explain the Corporation's motives in broadcasting the play. And then everything changed. The Duke of Edinburgh, in a speech at the Royal Society of Arts, came out in support of the production. On the morning of the Thursday when the play was due to be repeated in the evening, *The Times* newspaper leant its support as well, stating in its leader column:

Despite their use hundreds of times in newspapers, such phrases as 'totalitarianism', 'brain-washing', 'dangerous thoughts', and the Communist practice of making words stand on their heads have for millions of people taken on new meaning. The BBC is to be congratulated.

As a result, the repeat went out successfully four days after the initial outrage had broken out. The original concept for *Nineteen Eighty-Four* was of course George Orwell's, but once again Nigel Kneale had shown the way his brand of writing could affect the great television viewing public.

THE INVISIBLE MAN

In 1955, the BBC lost its monopoly on television broadcasting in Britain as ITV, the country's first commercial channel, took to the air. It wasn't just the advent of advertising between, and inserted into, the programmes that made ITV so different from the BBC, the new channel also offered a more populist style of entertainment that in many cases made the BBC seem staid. One such programme was *The Invisible Man*, broadcast from September 1958 to July 1959.

The idea was inspired by the H.G. Wells book of the same name published in 1897, but the storylines of the modern invisible man were a long way removed from Wells's Victorian anti-hero.

The plots revolved around Doctor Peter Brady who, while experimenting with light refraction as a method of achieving invisibility, is involved in an accident that makes him permanently invisible. The possibility of having an invisible man on its payroll is too much to resist for British Intelligence and it's not long before Brady is recruited as a British spy. At the same time, he uses his invisibility to help those in need.

In truth, the invisibility factor was the only real science fiction aspect of the series, which, once the existence of an invisible man was accepted, involved plots that revolved more around spy-cum-detective stories. A pilot episode was filmed in 1957, but was deemed unsuitable for transmission. Its problems were twofold.

First, in order to portray an invisible character, it was decided to wrap his head completely in bandages with two holes for his eyes, over which he wore sunglasses. He also wore gloves. In this way, the character was made visible to the audience. Unfortunately this meant the actor playing Brady had a tendency to bump into the props and scenery.

The second problem lay in scenes where he was meant to be invisible, meaning various props had to be moved as though by an invisible hand. This involved the use of fine wires meant to be indiscernible to the camera, but which were unfortunately very much in evidence a lot of the time.

A second pilot was subsequently made in which these problems were addressed and, for the day, many of the effects were impressive: an invisible Brady smoking a cigarette that seemed to hang in mid-air, or drinking wine from a glass, for example. Credit should also be given to the many actors who had to fake being hit, manhandled, thrown out of cars or just generally beaten up by someone who clearly wasn't there.

Because Brady's face was either invisible or covered in bandages, it was unnecessary to use the same actor for every episode, or even every scene in a single episode. Several actors were used and, at times, continuity was breached as Brady turned from slim to plump from scene to scene. When Brady was required to remove his bandages on screen, revealing what appeared to be a headless man in a suit, an extra small actor was employed whose head fell below Brady's collar as he looked out through buttonholes in his suit jacket. The actors who gave Brady a voice adopted mid-Atlantic accents in an effort to sell the serials to America. At the time of the transmissions, the actors who played or voiced Brady were never credited.

The Invisible Man ran for two series of thirteen episodes each. Run in their correct order, they told the story of how Brady's invisibility came about, how it was kept a secret, but later revealed to the public. Strangely, the networks that screened the serials sometimes chose to show them out of sequence, so that in one episode, everyone knew about Brady's invisibility, and in the next it was top secret.

Such things failed to kill the popularity of the programmes, which were still being repeated in the mid-1960s.

OTHER BRITISH TELEVISION SCIENCE FICTION

Although *Quatermass* is generally regarded as BBC Television's first adult science fiction serial, there were one-off plays and children's science fiction programmes before it, stretching back to the earliest days of television in 1938.

First in the 1950s was *Stranger From Space*, which began in October 1951 as part of *Whirligig*. This programme, first broadcast in 1950, was a children's variety show, known mostly for its resident puppets: Mr Turnip, Hank, Sooty and Sweep. *Stranger From Space* starred Bruce Beeby, who went on to play Mitch in BBC Radio's *Journey Into Space*. The stories concerned the adventures of Bilaphodorous, a Martian boy who crashes his Space Boat on Earth, where he meets schoolboy Ian Spencer. It was screened once a fortnight and young viewers were invited to write in with suggestions of how the adventures of Bilaphodorous and Michael might proceed.

More fantasy than true science fiction, *The Wonderful Visit*, shown as a one-off play in February 1952, was scripted by Nigel Kneale before he won fame as the creator of *Quatermass*. It was based on one of H.G. Wells's lesser-known stories, written in 1895, about a violin-playing angel who comes to Earth and is taken care of by a Vicar who has mistaken him for a bird and shot him. Not understanding the ways of our world, the angel becomes critical of much of what he sees, gets denounced as a Socialist and his host comes under attack from the locals for harbouring him. It was a strange little story to begin with, and the TV adaptation was not a great success. But the fantasy element of a mystical creature intermingling with the modern world was a subject that, for those who know his later works, was right up Nigel Kneale's street.

Kneale was also the writing force behind *Number Three*, a play televised in February 1953. This time the theme concerned a team of nuclear power scientists who come to realise that their leader is actually planning to use their research to build a weapon more devastating than the hydrogen bomb.

Actor Peter Cushing, who starred in a play called *Number Three*, then later in the notorious *Nineteen Eighty-Four* and *The Creature*, all scripted by Nigel Kneale. He is seen here in the 1958 movie *Dracula*.

Coming so close to the atom bombs dropped on Hiroshima and Nagasaki at the end of the Second World War, this was a subject that would have resonated heavily with viewers. Critics were not particularly impressed with *Number Three*, but it did give a small part to actor Peter Cushing, who would go on to star in the BBC's adaptation of *Nineteen Eighty-Four*.

In November 1953, a thirty-minute play called *Time Slip* was broadcast and, this time, Nigel Kneale was not the writer. *Time Slip* was written by Charles Eric Maine. He was an English author of science fiction and detective books whose career had begun earlier with the publication of a science fiction magazine called *The Satellite*, in which he published his own novels alongside the work of eminent writers of the day like Ray Bradbury. *Time Slip* was about a dead man who is brought back to life by a large shot of adrenalin, only to discover that his perception of time is a few seconds ahead of everyone else's, enabling him to answer questions before they are asked. The psychiatrist from whom he seeks help eventually cures him by killing him and then reviving him again, this time with a lesser shot of adrenalin.

January 1954 saw the arrival on television of Angus MacVicar's *The Lost Planet*, which had previously been broadcast on radio's *Children's Hour*.

It was followed, in January 1955, with the television version of *Return to the Lost Planet*. The plots followed similar lines to the aforementioned radio serials.

A one-off play called *The Voices* was televised in January 1955. Based on a novel called *Hero's Walk* by Robert Crane, it was set in 2021, when a world government is planning its next stage of space exploration. An artificial planet already orbits the Earth and another is planned for Mars. Further expansion is challenged when an alien force intervenes with threats of punishment to humans for trying to spread themselves too far into space. After a bit of political wrangling, the aliens back down and all ends well. At least, that's the way it was in the television play. In the book, from which it was adapted, the Earth is destroyed by the aliens.

By January 1955, Nigel Kneale was riding high following acclaim for his original screenplay for *The Quatermass Experiment* and his adaptation of *Nineteen Eighty-Four*. Success, then, seemed assured for Kneale's next production, called *The Creature*. One thing that the writer was very good at was latching on to current trends and interests and then writing a play that made strong associations. In January 1955, just a year and a half after the conquest of Everest, *The Creature* played on the public's perception of the existence of the Yeti, or Abominable Snowman (the title of the film made from the television play). Peter Cushing, fresh from his somewhat notorious success as Winston Smith in *Nineteen Eighty-Four*, took the role of Doctor John Rollason, who makes a journey to a remote monastery in Tibet – actually Alexandra Palace in North London – in search of the Yeti. The play created some interest, but nothing approaching the success and notoriety of either *Quatermass* or *Nineteen Eighty-Four*. In 1957, Hammer made a film version and Nigel Kneale once again wrote the script.

In January 1956, science fiction serials returned to children's television with the arrival of *Space School*. It concerned the three children of Space Commodore Hugh Sterling, whose job was to survey Mars, while his children stayed at home, living in a house on an orbiting satellite. The programme was soon lost to the memory of the few who watched it.

A one-off play called *The Critical Point* was broadcast in December 1957. Australian actor Leo McKern, later to find television fame as *Rumpole of the Bailey*, played scientist Andrew Mortimer who is involved with cryogenics. He has a partner in his experiments who kills his wife and, to escape the law, volunteers to be frozen in the hope of being resurrected at a later time when investigations into his crime might have been forgotten. Unfortunately, he fails to take into account the tenacity of a police inspector determined to bring him to justice. In the end, a mercy killing spares him his day in court. The play was fairly well received and repeated with a new cast in July 1960.

The decade ended on British television with three one-off adaptations rarely remembered today. *Doomsday for Dyson*, broadcast in 1958, was adapted from a story by J.B. Priestly. It concerned nuclear war and the dilemma of one man who is forced to kill his horrifically injured wife and daughter. *The Truth about Pyecraft*, in 1959, was adapted from a story by H.G. Wells, in which an obese man indulges in an occult recipe for weight loss, and ends up losing so much weight that, although still obese, he floats up to the ceiling of his house. Those who remember the presentation were impressed by the early special effects that made this happen. Also in 1959, an adaptation of a play called *The Offshore Island* involved a small family that survives a nuclear war after Europe has been devastated, leaving no more than a wasteland. Although science fiction played its part in the original premise, the play was more about humanity and politics and how both are affected by the devastation and after-effects of nuclear war.

Fourteen years after atom bombs were dropped on Hiroshima and Nagasaki, the nuclear nightmare still haunted the minds of storytellers, and the television viewing public alike.

MEANWHILE IN AMERICA

American television arrived for the masses a little ahead of its counterpart in Britain. Its science fiction serials, therefore, also began a little earlier. But by the 1950s, America and Britain each had its fair share of popular science fiction shows, although America, possibly spurred on by the commercial sponsors behind many shows, was more inclined to go for series and serials rather than one-off dramas.

Adventures of Superman

One of the greatest ever American science fiction heroes must surely be Superman. He was conceived back in the 1930s by Jerry Siegel and Joe Shuster, a writer and artist both working for DC Comics. The superhero made his debut in the first issue of *Action Comics* in June 1938, but it was 1952 before the Man of Steel made it to television.

For the few who do not know the Superman legend: He was born with the name Kal-El on the planet Krypton and sent by rocket to Earth as a baby by his father Jor-El, just before his home planet exploded. The conditions on Earth, compared to Krypton, gave him his superpowers. He was found and adopted by Jonathan and Martha Kent in Smallville, where he took on his secret identity as Clark Kent. When he grew up, he moved to the city of Metropolis, where, as Clark Kent, he took a job as a reporter on *The Daily Planet* newspaper, keeping his superpowers a secret while, in his Superman guise, using them to help people and prevent all kinds of tragedies and disasters whenever and wherever he was needed. As Clark Kent, he enjoyed a platonic relationship with fellow reporter Lois Lane, who was in love with Superman without ever realising that he and Clark were actually the same person.

Superman arrived on television in a 1951 black and white film called *Superman and the Mole Men*, later broadcast as a two-part serial in the television series under the title *The Unknown People*. The plot revolved around Clark and Lois being sent to a town called Silsby to cover a story about the drilling of the world's deepest oil well. What the drillers fail to realise is that their drill has penetrated the home of a race of underground beings, who then come up to the surface and scare the townsfolk of Silsby by glowing in the dark. Naturally, as is often the case in science fiction stories, the people of the town rise up to destroy the interlopers. Only Superman, once Clark has managed to give Louis the slip, can save the situation. Which he does, and peace is regained.

Superman and the Mole Men was a two-part story, which kicked off the series that ran on American television until 1958, from 1952 to 1954 in black and white, and 1954 to 1958 in colour. As was often the case, the series sparked the release of various promotional items, designed to attract young viewers.

The part of Superman was played by George Reeves, coincidentally a surname remarkably similar to that of Christopher Reeve who would play the superhero so successfully on screen in 1978. As with most science fiction productions of the 1950s, the biggest challenge lay in the special effects.

From the days when George Reeves played Superman, an American toy horseshoe game that tied its name to the show.

Shows of super strength could be easily faked with rubber 'iron' bars and the like, but Superman's main claim to fame was his flying ability, and each episode needed a good helping of the hero taking off, flying and landing. Early take-offs were facilitated by Reeves hanging from wires; later an out-of-camera-range springboard was used for him to bounce into the air. Landing came about by the actor jumping from a ladder or being lowered by an off-camera bar. For the flying sequences, Reeves lay along a thin board that had

George Reeves in his American television Superman guise meets a rather unconvincing robot.

been moulded to his body shape as scenery or back-projected footage rushed past him.

For Reeves, winning the part of Superman was both a blessing and a curse. His early claim to fame had been as one of Scarlett O'Hara's suitors in *Gone with the Wind*. Interrupted by a spell in the US Army, various film roles followed, including a small part in *From Here to Eternity*. *Superman* shot him to fame, but he became heavily typecast by it, so much so that he even played the part in other shows such as *I Love Lucy*, a popular American comedy series starring Lucille Ball. Reeves died from a gunshot to his head in 1959. Suicide was suspected but never proved and not fully accepted by friends and fellow actors.

Anthologies

One thing America's science fiction television caught on to before British television was the use of the anthology: one generic name for a series of programmes, each with a different storyline and different actors, but all connected by their use of science fiction themes.

By the start of the 1950s, science fiction cinema films had taken on a more adult approach to plots, epitomised perhaps by *The Day the Earth Stood Still* in 1951. At the same time, authors like Isaac Asimov and Robert Heinlein in America and John Wyndham in Britain were also writing the kind of science fiction appreciated more by an adult rather than the more juvenile audience that was previously targeted. In America, the television science fiction anthologies followed this trend.

The first in the 1950s was *Tales of Tomorrow*, which began in 1951 and ran for more than eighty episodes until 1953. Short stories by well-known science fiction authors of the day were adapted for television, along with abridged versions of classic novels that included *Frankenstein* and *20,000 Leagues Under the Sea*. Neither was the series short of famous names in its cast lists, Paul Newman, Lon Chaney, Rod Steiger and Veronica Lake being just a few of the names that acted in the various stories.

Tales of Tomorrow was replaced by *Science Fiction Theatre*, which began in 1955 and ran for more than seventy episodes until 1957. This anthology series dwelt more on stories whose plots were based in then current scientific discoveries, or how such discoveries might be extrapolated to include subjects like alien invasion, telepathy, robots and even time travel.

Perhaps the most famous of the American anthologies, which later found fame on British television, was *The Twilight Zone*, which began in America in 1959 and ran for five years. It was epitomised by an introduction to each episode spoken by Rod Serling, an American actor, screenwriter and TV producer. He was particularly famous for a series of quotes that began each show and set the eerie tone for what was to follow. Here are some examples.

> There is a fifth dimension, beyond that which is known to man. It is a dimension as vast as space and as timeless as infinity. It is the middle ground between light and shadow, between science and superstition.

> It may be said with a degree of assurance that not everything that meets the eye is as it appears.

> Imagination … its limits are only those of the mind itself.

Other American science fiction

Anthologies aside, American television of the 1950s also broadcast several science fiction serials, although before the advent of the anthologies, these were mostly aimed at younger viewers.

Buck Rogers, the space pilot made famous on radio and comic strips, made it to television in 1950 and the series named after the character ran for thirty-nine episodes until 1951, generating promotional toys for children of the decade for several years after. A series featuring a similar hero, in the shape of Flash Gordon, also ran for thirty-nine episodes from 1953 to 1954.

At the same time, *Captain Video*, which had begun in 1949, was still surviving and continued to survive until 1955. Using some of the new technologies available and falling back on filmed inserts between live action, it proved popular, even though many of its storylines would be considered somewhat banal today.

Cashing in on the way that younger viewers enjoyed joining clubs or buying merchandise connected with their favourite shows, American science fiction took its viewers to places that non-commercial British channels like the BBC could not hope to copy. With that in mind, heavily sponsored shows like *Tom Corbett Space Cadet* and *Space Patrol* made the progression from radio to television. The first was about a space academy where members of

A toy Buck Rogers Sonic Ray Gun, made by the American Norton-Honer Manufacturing Company in the mid-1950s.

the Solar Guard trained and visited alien worlds. The second was set in the thirtieth century as its hero Buzz Corry thwarted the evil plans of villains from around the Universe. Another series, *Rod Brown of the Rocket Rangers*, tried its luck, but had to be cancelled because of its claimed similarity to *Tom Corbett Space Cadet*. Two more shows, which began life on regional TV and eventually made it to national syndication, were *Captain Z-Ro*, whose time machine allowed him to take a look at history, which sometimes turned out different from what he had expected, and *Rocky Jones, Space Ranger*, whose hero was head of a kind of interplanetary police force.

It was juvenile series like these, and the more adult-themed anthologies, that eventually led to the now legendary *Star Trek*, which debuted in September 1966. But that's another story.

Chapter Three

Science Fiction on Film

Anyone who grew up in the 1950s with an insatiable appetite for science fiction soon came up against one major stumbling block when it came to the cinema: the dreaded 'X' certificate.

All films went before the British Board of Film Censors, which was created as far back as 1912. Before any film was allowed to be released into the cinema, the Board viewed it and awarded it a certificate. In the 1950s, there were three classifications. The 'U' certificate meant the film was good family viewing and anyone could see it. The 'A' certificate meant children were allowed into the cinema but only when accompanied by an adult. Up until the start of the 1950s there had also been the 'H' certificate, which was primarily awarded to horror films. But in 1951, ironically timed right when the cinema was about to enjoy a huge boom in science fiction, the 'X' certificate was created. It decreed that no one under the age of sixteen was

The dreaded 'X' certificate issued by the British Board of Film Censors to so many of the science fiction films of the 1950s.

allowed to see the film. Today, many of those old 'X' certificate films are regularly shown on daytime television, but back then, if the British Board of Film Censors members even got a sniff of a monster, an 'X' certificate was inevitable.

If you were tall for your age or looked older than your years, it was possible sneak into an 'X' certificate film, but it was a daunting experience. First you had to get past the cinema's commissionaire. He was usually an old man with a long coat and a peaked hat whose job was to open the doors for the cinema goers and control the queues on Saturday nights, the busiest night of the week when there were usually more prospective patrons than seats in the average cinema. Once passed the commissionaire, you were faced with the lady in the ticket-selling booth – and she could spot anyone under the age of sixteen at a hundred paces. Assuming you made it past the commissionaire and the ticket booth lady, your final obstacle was the usherette who, torch in hand, showed you to your seat. Back in those days, even if you were sixteen, getting into an 'X' certificate film was not for the weak-hearted.

Plot influences

Occasionally in Britain, but chiefly in America and sometimes Japan, something like 200 science fiction films were made between 1950 and 1959. That works out at more than one and a half films per month over a period of ten years. Four factors largely influenced this huge outpouring.

1. The Second World War, which ended five years before the start of the decade, had seen major advances in scientific research, and many of the resulting discoveries, made public for the first time, showed that what had once seemed impossible to be a lot more feasible, especially when exaggerated by science fiction film makers.
2. The end of the war was marked by atomic bombs dropped on Hiroshima and Nagasaki in 1945, with devastating consequences. As a result, words like 'atom', 'atomic' and 'radio activity' entered the common language. In the major film studios such words became synonymous with horror, disfiguration and anything that might be transformed from the mundane into the truly dreadful. It was a rule of science fiction films of the 1950s that something that was transformed or created as a result of anything even vaguely atomic or radioactive was not good for mankind.

3. Following the Second World War, the political climate changed to a cold war, in particular between America and Russia. Despite being on the same side during the previous conflict, the two countries held very different political views: America, the land of the free; Russia, a country dominated by communism. Public awareness of communism in America was very much tied in with brainwashing and the fear of being taken over. Substitute aliens for Russians and you have the basis for a great many American science fiction films of the 1950s, in which people's minds and bodies were taken over by something nasty.

4. In June 1947, the first post-war sighting of unidentified flying objects (UFOs), otherwise known as flying saucers, was made by an American private aircraft pilot who reported seeing nine shiny objects travelling at what he estimated to be about 120 miles per hour past a mountain in Washington State. There had been sightings before, but this one really roused the public's interest. Further flying saucer sightings continued over the next few weeks and then sporadically until the mid-1950s. The sightings became another major influence in the plotting of science fiction films of the time.

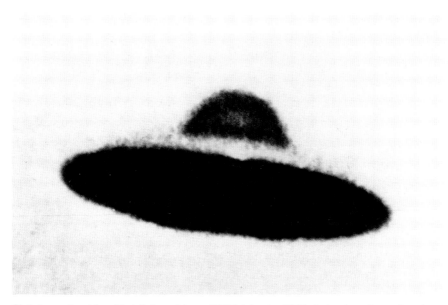

Sightings of unidentified flying objects (UFOs) in the 1950s helped to shape the plots of many of the decade's films. This picture was taken in New Jersey, USA on 28 July 1952, and was later authenticated by British UFO experts.

Plot stereotypes

Although the decade saw a good many sensible, well thought-out, highly feasible and intelligent stories, it must be said that there were a great more stereotypical films that fell a good way short of that ideal. Many of these could be placed in one of four categories.

1. **A Biblical prophecy come true in our own lifetime.** At some point in this plotline, at least one character could be guaranteed to utter those words. This is the straightforward end of the world story, a situation from which it is absolutely impossible for the characters to have any form of escape. The world is going to end and that's that. Unless of course … and there's always an *unless* that is discovered by someone that no one else believes until he or she battles bureaucracy and foolish army majors to do whatever is needed to save the world before the final credits.

2. **The end of civilisation as we have come to know it.** This isn't quite the end of the world. With just a few exceptions, every man, woman and child has been struck blind, poisonous plants may well have uprooted and begun to stalk the countryside in search of victims, a nasty plague has undoubtedly decimated the best part of the planet, or maybe 90 per cent of the population has turned into zombies – and it's all because some fool has been messing about with something atomic. A few brave souls, however, have survived to spend the next ninety minutes or so building a new form of civilization. As the hero and heroine, in the closing scene of the film, gaze into the last rays of the setting sun, they look into each other's eyes and vow that this time things will be different. Cue the final credits which state: 'THE END … of the beginning'.

3. **My God what was that?** Usually it's something very big, very green and very angry. It's a monster that has been woken from hibernation in the Arctic wastes by a misguided scientist with – you guessed it – an atom bomb, or an atomic ray, or at least something with vaguely atomic connections, and now that the monster is awake it won't be content until it has destroyed at least one major city of the world. This plot usually contains an earnest scientist who thinks the monster should be kept alive, a beautiful girl with whom the monster is gentle, and an army general who only wants to blow the thing to kingdom come.

4. **Daddy, what's that strange bump on the back of your neck?** Also known as *Charlie, what's that strange look in your eyes?* and *Mummy, why does your voice sound so strange?* Whether it's the voice, their eyes or nothing more than a funny bump on the neck, Mummy, Daddy and Charlie all have one thing in common: they have been taken over by an alien being. This was a very common theme in some of the best and also

In the 1954 Japanese film, Godzilla was a monster that evolved from an ancient sea creature disturbed by atomic bomb tests.

some of the worst science fiction films of the 1950s, possibly because it was a lot cheaper for an ordinary actor to exhibit a glazed look, strange voice or neck bump than it was for the film company to actually build an alien being.

Another dimension

The launch of so many science fiction films in the 1950s neatly coincided with a renewed interest in 3-D photography and film-making. The reason why we see the world in three dimensions is that the brain takes the two slightly different views seen by each of our eyes, compares them and combines them to give the illusion of depth in a single image.

It was the same with films that were shot using special cameras with twin lenses that produced two pictures with slightly different perspectives. Viewed in the normal way, the screen showed two different images, one red and the other green, slightly misplaced in relation to each other. The audience then watched the film while wearing what were known technically as anaglyph glasses. These were actually little more than pieces of cardboard with two 'lenses' made from thin sheets of transparent plastic, one red and the other green. In this way the left eye, looking through the red lens, and the right eye, viewing the film through the green lens, saw two slightly different images. The brain did its magic and the audience got an impression

3-D anaglyph glasses, like those used by cinema audiences of the 1950s.

of depth, with objects appearing to hurtle out of the screen towards them or recede into exaggeratedly far distances. It was the perfect medium for science fiction films.

Poster misconceptions

Another common aspect of a great many 1950s science fiction films was the misleading interpretations that might be had from the posters that advertised them. Many bore little or no resemblance to the films they were advertising. While they usually depicted the main characters, they did so in ways that had little to do with the actual plots and a lot to do with showing beautiful girls in various states of undress being menaced by monsters and mad scientists.

A classic case in point is the poster for *Forbidden Planet*, one of the more intelligent films of the era, which featured Robby the Robot. Robby was a benign robot. At one point in the film, his scientist owner directs him to shoot someone and his circuits go into meltdown. It is impossible, it seems, for Robby to do any harm to a human, especially to the beautiful daughter of the scientist. And yet, on the poster for *Forbidden Planet*, there he is, with what appear to be huge, glowing red eyes as he strides across an alien landscape with the lovely and scantily clad daughter in his menacing metal arms.

Forbidden Planet was not alone in this particular form of transgression. There was the poster for *The Day the Earth Stood Still*, with its huge robot destroying everything in its path, whilst carrying off a beautiful woman who bore no resemblance whatsoever to any actress in the film; there was *Invaders from Mars*, with its enormous green Martian carrying away another apparently unconscious woman; there was *Invasion of the Saucer-Men* with its huge-headed, green, bug-eyed monsters manhandling yet another woman whose dress only just about covered her decency … the list goes on. It's no wonder that so many films, with perfectly innocent themes ended up with 'X' certificates.

What follows is nothing like a comprehensive round-up of every science fiction film made in the decade. It is more a personal look at what I consider to be some of the best and some of the worst. And if you are anything like me, you'll agree that even the bad films were good in their own ways.

1950: DESTINATION MOON

Destination Moon is the film that is usually reckoned to have been responsible for starting the 1950s science fiction boom. It was directed by George Pal, a Hungarian who made his name in France as an animator before moving to America, where he became a producer and director, principally of science fiction films. The film was loosely based on a novel called *Rocketship Galileo* by Robert Heinlein, a popular and sometimes controversial science fiction writer of the time, who was also one the three screenplay writers on the film.

Although cloaked in fiction, *Destination Moon* was practically a documentary concerning the first manned flight to the moon, as was made clear in the studio's publicity at the time:

Destination Moon is a projection documentary of man's greatest dream: A visit to the moon. In no way treated as a fantasy or as a 'Buck Rogers type' epic, this Technicolor film story follows the indications of the latest works and discoveries of today's top scientists.

How film-makers saw the rocket launch command centre in *Destination Moon.*

It was also an indication of how Americans at that time harboured a preoccupation with the Russians and the prevention of their getting to the Moon first and establishing a military base.

For its time, the film's special effects were convincing, especially in the creation of the lunar landscape and the sequence in which one of the crew finds himself adrift in space. That said, the film's depiction of the command centre that controlled the rocket's launch was a very long way removed from the real thing that would be seen on television during the actual moon landings less than twenty years later.

Nevertheless, the film was as scientifically accurate as possible. It relied not only Heinlein's own knowledge, but also on the expertise of German rocket expert Herman Oberth. His interests in rockets began as a child when he was given a copy of *From the Earth to the Moon* by Jules Verne and worked out for himself that Verne's calculations were based in fact. At the early age of fourteen he had developed a theory for rocket propulsion and in 1923 he proved that it would be possible to put a man into space using rocket power. By the time he acted as an adviser on *Destination Moon*, Oberth had become known as the Father of Rocketry.

Unfortunately, in the world of entertainment, accuracy isn't always as important as entertainment. At the end of the day, the film was accurate, worthy and a little dull.

Perhaps that dullness was the reason why, all too often, producers of the day ceased using established science fiction authors to script their movies and turned instead to more established screenplay writers who understood the mechanics of plotting rather better than they understood the mechanics of a rocket. The result was that many of the films of the time were vastly entertaining but scientifically poor.

1951: THE DAY THE EARTH STOOD STILL

The Day the Earth Stood Still was directed by Robert Wise, who went on to win an Academy Award for his direction of *West Side Story*. It was based on a short story called *Farewell to the Master* by American science fiction writer and editor Harry Bates. The atmospheric music was by Bernard Herrmann, who later wrote the terrifying music score for Alfred Hitchcock's *Psycho*.

A flying saucer approaches the Earth and lands in Washington. It is encircled by the army, ready for trouble. An opening appears in the saucer's side and out steps a tall, slender man. He looks human, but he is an alien named Klaatu, perfectly played by the British stage, television and film actor Michael Rennie. He is accompanied by a huge, silent robot called Gort.

Klaatu explains that he wishes to meet all world leaders in one place and that he has a message for them. When he produces a small device, a nearby soldier thinks it is a weapon and shoots him. Gort springs into action and melts the soldier's weapon with a ray from his eyes.

After some minor surgery, Klaatu pursues his quest to meet with world leaders while the army attempts to break into his saucer. Neither have any great success. With the help of a young boy – another mainstay of 1950s science fiction films – Klaatu eventually gets to meet a scientist and to explain something about his mission. It seems people from other planets are worried about the fact that Earth has started to develop atomic power.

The scientist suggests that Klaatu gives a demonstration of his powers. So, for twenty-four hours, he neutralizes electricity all over the Earth, with the exception of that supplied to hospitals and used by planes in flight. This is the day the Earth stands still.

Klaatu meets an Earth woman called Helen. He tells her if anything should happen to him, Gort will begin the destruction of Earth and, if that is the case, only she can stop him by uttering the words 'Klaatu barada nikto' within the robot's earshot. Inevitably, Klaatu gets shot, Helen races to the saucer, Gort begins his rampage and Helen stops him with the three words Klaatu has taught her. Gort carries her into the saucer and goes in search of Klaatu's body, which he also brings to the saucer.

Brought back to life temporarily, but only long enough to give the people of Earth his message, Klaatu explains to anyone who will listen that he is part of an interplanetary organisation that uses invincible robots like Gort to patrol planets and preserve peace by the simple expedient of annihilating any aggressors. This is how the planets in Klaatu's organisation keep peace among themselves.

As Helen is released, Klaatu leaves mankind with one simple message: 'If you threaten to extend your violence, this Earth of yours will be reduced to a burned-out cinder. Your choice is simple. Join us and live in peace, or pursue your present course and face obliteration. We will be awaiting your answer. The decision rests with you.' And with that, he's off, back in his saucer and away into space.

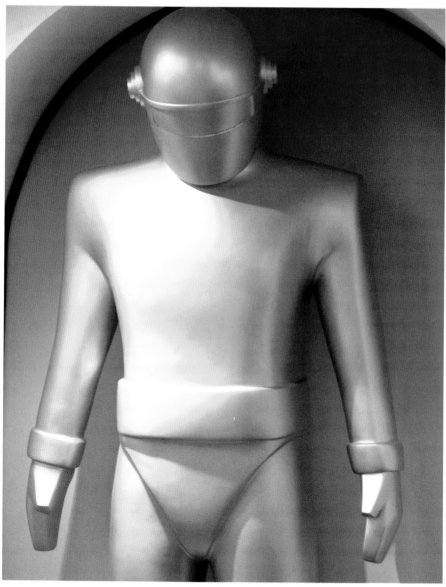

A replica of Gort, the robot in *The Day the Earth Stood Still*, on display at the Robot Hall of Fame in Pennsylvania.

Made in black and white, with a dramatic use of light and shadows, *The Day the Earth Stood Still* has everything a good 1950s science fiction film should have: a benign but misunderstood alien, a flying saucer, a rampaging robot, destructive rays, references to atomic power and a nod towards the paranoia of an audience for whom the Second World War had ended only six years before.

The film was remade in 2008 with Keanu Reeves as Klaatu. The new version was in colour, the special effects were impressive, but the sentimentality of the altered plot reduced the power of the original.

1953: INVADERS FROM MARS

Invaders from Mars was directed by William Cameron Menzies, better known as a Hollywood art director who had worked on such classics as *Gone with the Wind* and *The Thief of Baghdad* in 1924 and 1940 respectively.

The film was originally made in garishly coloured 3-D. As such, when seen today in its more traditional 2-D version, it seems too full of strange camera angles, set pieces with great depth, such as long corridors, and objects that tend to advance unexpectedly towards the camera – all tricks of the three-dimensional cinematographer's art.

Invaders from Mars starts with 12-year-old David MacLean looking out of his bedroom window in the night and seeing a strange green flying saucer that is apparently landing in a sandpit some way from his house.

The Martians have landed, buried themselves under the earth and are capturing people by swallowing them up through a whirlpool of sand, a fairly regular event that happens in conjunction with the sound of heavenly voices. The audience could have been forgiven for believing that the voices were there only for effect, as part of the background music that never seems to cease its weird harmonies in science fiction films of the 1950s. But they would have been wrong. 'It's that music again,' says one of the characters just before the ground opens and swallows another victim, destined like all the others to be operated on below ground and to return a little later with a lack of emotion and a small bump on the back of the neck.

It's a fate that befalls David's dad quite early in the film. When his mum calls in two policemen to investigate the disappearance of her husband, it's not long before all three return with bumps on their necks and a complete lack of emotion. So of course, it's up to David to save the world.

Invaders from Mars takes on board all the basics of classic 1950s science fiction: invasion by flying saucers, minds being taken over by unknown entities and a suspicion of things that might be radioactive. There is a lot of talk about rays. Just what, for instance, are the Martians using to build their underground fortress?

'Some sort of a ray,' says one of the characters.

'Like an X-ray?' asks another.

'Yes, some sort of radioactive ray that could smash through the Earth. Or a transmitter that could manufacture infrared rays that could melt through the Earth.'

Once David has spent the first half of the film trying to convince all the grown-ups that those bumps on the back of people's necks are something more than gnat bites, the army arrives on stock footage to fight the Martians. But even they have their reservations about rays.

'If they've got a ray down there I don't know what good our tanks are gonna do,' says one of the soldiers.

In the end the day is saved by David who, having faced the head Martian, described as mankind developed to its ultimate intelligence but who resembles nothing as much as a head with tentacles in a goldfish bowl, leads the troops through the labyrinth of underground tunnels built by the Martians until they come to a dead end.

'If only we had an infrared ray to burn through all this rock,' says one of the soldiers, and, as luck would have it, they find one just a few paces on.

So the soldiers battle the Martians and they blow up the flying saucer and they all flee back to the surface and, before you know it, David is back in bed. Much to his relief, it turns out it was all a dream. But then he happens to glance out of his window. Outside, a strange green flying saucer is descending from the sky. Cue the final credits.

1953: THE WAR OF THE WORLDS

The story of alien invasion in 1950s science fiction is often said to have been inspired by the climate of the Cold War at that time. But the original story of *The War of the Worlds*, on which the 1953 film was based, was written by H.G. Wells, serialised in magazines in the UK and America in 1897 and published as a novel in 1898.

That said, the age in which it was written had its own fears and prejudices, which influenced Wells's story in ways not dissimilar to those of the era in which the story was rewritten for the cinema by British journalist and

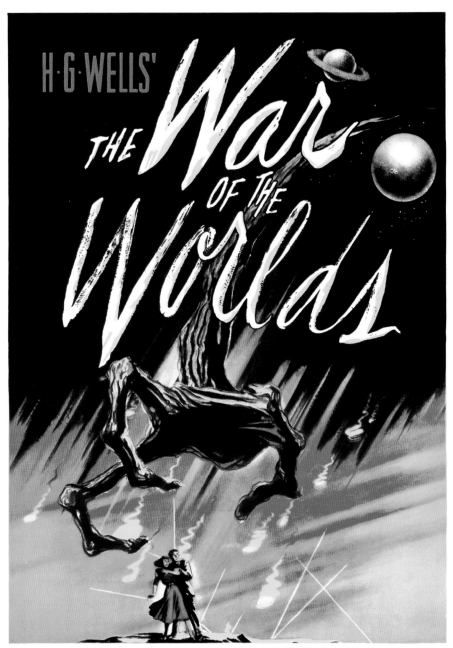

The poster for *The War of the Worlds.*

short story writer turned playwright and screenwriter Barré Lyndon. The film was produced by George Pal, who had previously directed *Destination Moon*, and directed by Byron Haskin, a former special effects artist.

The unnamed journalist who narrates the story in the book becomes Doctor Clayton Forrester in the film, played by Gene Barry, who later won fame as the title character in US TV series *Burke's Law*.

Modern-day Woking in Surrey, where Wells's story is commemorated by a huge metal sculpture of a Martian fighting machine.

The original novel was set in Victorian Surrey and London, and is commemorated today with a huge metal sculpture of a Martian fighting machine that towers over pedestrians and traffic in Wells's home town of Woking, whose destruction by the Martians is graphically described in the original story. The film, however, in true Hollywood style, shifts the action to 1950s Los Angeles, and the three-legged fighting machines that strode across the countryside in the novel are replaced by hovering, saucer-shaped ships from which a lens on a long pod dispenses death rays to anyone or anything unlucky enough to get in its sights.

The War of the Worlds is often lauded as one of the greats of 1950s science fiction, and it still stands up remarkably well today. But, at its core, it is a fairly predictable story of the Martians arriving, and slowly advancing across the country, killing and destroying everything in their path, driving humanity before them, as the inadequate weapons of the world's armies fail to fight back.

The special effects are mostly impressive, but would have been better if budget constrictions had not intervened. The plan had been to shoot part of the film, showing the destruction of major cities of the world, in 3-D. But with a dwindling budget, this was replaced with stock footage from Second World War newsreels. Maybe the tight budget was also responsible for the fact that the Martian ships that hung so menacingly above Lost Angeles did so by means of what were often all too visible wires.

As Doctor Forrester spends best part of the film fleeing, hiding and calculating ways to beat the Martians, his job is eventually done for him by all the bacteria that is common in the Earth's atmosphere, and to which the Martians have no resistance. In the end, the common germs in the air to which Earth people are immune kill off all the Martians. This was the way Wells wrote his ending in the book.

War of the Worlds (without the definite article that was part of the title of both the book and the earlier film) was remade in 2005, starring Tom Cruise and directed by Steven Spielberg. Although the story deviated from both the book and the earlier film, the basic underlying theme – and the design of the Martian fighting machines – was the closer of the two films to Wells's original concept.

1953: IT CAME FROM OUTER SPACE

The title and the posters for *It Came from Outer Space* promised a lot more than the film delivered: *Amazing, Exciting, Spectacular; Fantastic sights leap at you; How can you escape from a sight you cannot see, from a fear you cannot face?* The message was reinforced by the fact that the film was made in 3-D. Audiences, however, found it less frightening than most of its time. Instead, they discovered a well thought-out film with a few shocks, but not as many really scary moments as they had been promised.

The film had a better pedigree than most. Written by Harry Essex, an ex-journalist and short story writer for distinguished American magazines like *Saturday Evening Post* and *Colliers*, it was based on a story by American fantasy and science fiction writer Ray Bradbury, who was winning acclaim at this time as author of *The Martian Chronicles*. The film starred Richard

The poster for *It Came from Outer Space*.

Carlson, who later appeared in the classic *Creature from the Black Lagoon* and less well-known *The Magnetic Monster*. It was directed by Jack Arnold who, four years later, would go on to direct *The Incredible Shrinking Man*.

At its heart, *It Came from Outer Space* is a good old alien takeover story, as inhabitants of a small town in Arizona begin behaving strangely following the crashing of a huge meteorite in the nearby desert. Amateur astronomer John Putnam investigates the crash and discovers it is actually an alien spaceship that has buried itself deep underground.

The alien takeover, however, isn't what it appears to be. Unlike most science fiction films of the 1950s, the aliens don't want to take over the world. It transpires they have crash-landed by accident and plan to stay on Earth only for the amount of time needed to repair their ship. The only reason why they have begun taking over the minds of the local inhabitants is to exert the influence needed to persuade the townsfolk to gather materials and help with the repairs.

Other than that, the aliens are peaceful. They are, of course, also misunderstood. So when the people from the town rise up and form a posse to seek out and destroy the interlopers, it's up to Putnam to protect them and delay the impending violence just long enough for the spaceship repairs to be carried out and for the aliens to make good their escape. Whereupon, all the people who have been helping while under the influence of alien mind control are set free and return to normal.

Critical reaction when the film was released was not overly enthusiastic, but since then it has become a classic which, unusually for a 1950s science fiction story, portrays the inhuman aliens as possessing an unexpected degree of humanity.

1955: THIS ISLAND EARTH

Hurtling through outer space, they challenged the unearthly furies of an outlaw planet, screamed the posters for *This Island Earth*, which began life as a novel by American science fiction writer Raymond F. Jones. It was published during 1952 in three parts in consecutive editions of *Thrilling Wonder Stories*. In 1955, the novel was adapted for the cinema and released by Universal. Critics of the time praised it for its amazing and colourful special effects.

Rex Reason, who began his career on the stage and later went on to star in the television series *The Roaring Twenties*, played scientist Cal Meacham.

The poster for *This Island Earth*.

He is also a jet aircraft pilot who is saved from crashing by an eerie green glow in the sky. It seems the aliens who saved him need him for something more. From a mysterious unknown source he receives plans for some kind of communications device called an interocitor.

Naturally he can't resist building it and turning it on, only to find himself faced, on the device's screen, by an alien, who tells him that building the interocitor was a test of his abilities. He is invited to join other scientists with similar abilities and intellects, one of whom, luckily for the plot, is an ex-girlfriend of Cal's called Ruth.

After a few plot twists and turns in which there are escapes, captures and general incineration of superfluous cast members, Cal and Ruth board a plane, which is beamed up into a flying saucer and taken to the planet Metaluna. The planet is under attack by Zagons, who are sending meteorites to destroy the Metaluna atmosphere. For that reason, the Metalunans intend to journey to Earth and set up new lives there.

Cal and Ruth of course are not too keen on the plan, but the Metalunans have other ideas. A quick trip to their Thought Transference Chamber will rob the Earth couple of their free will.

They do, however, have one Metalunan on their side. His name is Exeter, and he helps them escape, although he is injured by a Zagon mutant while trying to get to the flying saucer that will take them all to Earth. The subsequent scenes of the saucer flying through the meteor bombardment just above the erupting surface of the planet are among some of the best special effects in any science fiction film of the 1950s.

As the saucer breaks free, Metaluna's ionization layer finally fractures under the Zagon bombardment and, as is so often the case at the end of 1950s science fiction films, the planet explodes. Luckily, the aircraft in which Cal and Ruth began their adventure is on the saucer in which they are travelling. The get in, fly out and make their escape. The badly injured Exeter isn't so fortunate. Declining their offer to join them on Earth, he flies the saucer out over the ocean, where it erupts into a ball of flame.

Posters of the time claimed the film was two and a half years in the making, 'to bring you sights of fantastic amazement never before possible on the motion picture screen'. A little over the top maybe, but it was one of the better science fiction films of the 1950s.

1956: INVASION OF THE BODY SNATCHERS

One of the best films of the era and one that handled the alien takeover theme to perfection was *Invasion of the Body Snatchers*, a truly dreadful title for one of the best science fiction films of all time. It was directed by Don Sigel who, although born in Chicago, was educated at Cambridge University in England. He had already won two Academy Awards in 1945 for a couple of short films and was known for some of the better-than-usual, well-crafted 'B' pictures of the time before directing *Invasion of the Body Snatchers*. It was adapted from a story written by American author Jack Finney, already well known for his intelligent science fiction novels and short stories.

The plot concerns the mysterious arrival of pods from outer space which give birth to, and then replace, human beings who fall asleep in their near vicinity. Made in black and white, the film combines the use of crooked camera angles, strongly directional lighting and powerful background music to emphasise the events of the story.

Pacing throughout is perfect. The film has been running for forty minutes before the audience even sees one of the pods and, by then, they are nicely ready for its true horror. The hero and heroine are Miles Bennel and his girlfriend Becky, played by Kevin McCarthy and Dana Wynter, with the action set in the fictional Californian town of Santa Mira.

There is some wonderful dialogue from screenplay writer Daniel Mainwaring, an ex-newspaper journalist turned mystery writer, who was aided by an uncredited Sam Peckinpah, the man who later won a reputation for blood-thirsty films that included *The Wild Bunch* in 1969 and the notorious *Straw Dogs* in 1971.

'We can't close our eyes all night,' Miles tells Becky, as more and more of the population of Santa Mira comes under the influence of the pods. 'We'll wake up changed into something inhuman. Only when we have to fight to stay human do we realise how dear it is to us.'

Unfortunately Becky doesn't fight quite as hard as her boyfriend. She sleeps and is taken over. Miles, not realising the truth, kisses her and, as he says later, 'I didn't know the real meaning of fear until I kissed Becky.'

Invasion of the Body Snatchers is full to overflowing with good solid paranoia as Miles battles to make himself believed, only to see more and more of his friends going under.

The film ends on an upbeat as he eventually makes it to a hospital where his story is accepted and the authorities swing into action. But that's not the way the director wanted it. The story was originally written to end with a scene still in the film but now some minutes before the official ending, in which Miles staggers distraught from lack of sleep onto a dark highway ranting about the pods to drivers of speeding cars, trying to stop them, demanding help and endeavouring in vain to make himself understood as he cries to deaf ears, 'They're here already ... and your next!'

Invasion of the Body Snatchers was remade under the same title in 1978 and the result, while not quite as creepy as the first version, was still a very good and sometimes disturbing film. A third version, made in 1993 under the shortened title *Body Snatchers*, never quite captured the menace of the original.

1956: FORBIDDEN PLANET

Forbidden Planet was one of the best science fiction films of the 1950s, with an intelligent and imaginative plot, believable characters and impressive special effects. It was also the film that introduced audiences to one of science fiction's most memorable and best-loved characters: Robby the Robot.

Robby was a mechanical marvel that a great many filmgoers believed to be a real automaton. In fact, like so many other non-human science fiction characters before and after him, Robby was actually a man (or several men during his film-making lifetime) dressed up. But he was dressed to perfection.

Standing at more than 7 feet in height, Robby was designed by Robert Kinoshita, a Japanese–American engineer, and built by the MGM props department. The reported cost was $125,000. Contrary to what appeared to be the case on the film poster for *Forbidden Planet*, he did not have eyes as such. Instead, his swivelling 'head' culminated in a huge transparent dome in which various relays could be seen and heard clicking and clacking, with two revolving antennae, which protruded from each side.

His voice seemed to come from his mid section, which was accompanied by a blue flashing grill between his arms, which extended each side and ended in twin-digit clawlike hands. His legs were a series of flexible rings that allowed him to sort of waddle along rather than walk. In *Forbidden Planet*, the uncredited actor inside Robby was Frankie Darro, whose parents were circus aerialists, and who was noted for his small stature and ability to perform his own stunts.

The film was directed by Fred McLeod Wilcox, best known until then for a sentimental film called *Lassie Come Home*. The screenplay was written by novelist Cyril Hume, who is said to have taken elements of the plot from Shakespeare's *The Tempest*. Also credited for the original story were writers Irving Block and Allen Adler. Few of those who saw the film would have made the connection with Shakespeare.

The action takes place on the planet Altair-4, where scientist Edward Morbius lives with his beautiful, and usually scantily clad, daughter Altaira. Together with their faithful robot Robbie, they are the sole survivors of a colonization attempt that went wrong when everyone but the scientist, his beautiful daughter and faithful robot were killed by some strange malevolent force. As the film starts, Commander Adams – played by Leslie Nielsen, later to find fame in the *Naked Gun* comedy film series – arrives in a flying saucer-shaped spaceship on a mission to rescue the survivors.

The poster for *Forbidden Planet*.

A replica of Robby the Robot, built from the blueprints used to create the original robot for *Forbidden Planet*.

The original Robby makes an appearance at San Diego Comic Con in 2006, in honour of the 50th anniversary of *Forbidden Planet*.

The newcomers are not welcome. Morbius wants to stay, Altaira doesn't know any other life and Robby does whatever he's told. To make matters worse, the malevolent force rears its head again, this time attacking the rescue mission crew.

It transpires that the reason why Morbius doesn't want to leave is because he has found an amazingly vast underground city, built by the planet's now extinct occupants, the Krell. They had superhuman intellects that had built a machine capable of turning thoughts into reality. While experimenting with the Krell machinery Morbius has boosted his own intellect and now he can use their machine. He discovers that the combination of their super-brains and the machine that could turn their thoughts into substance was enough to wipe out their entire civilisation.

The problem, of course, is that although the Krell have gone, their machines remain and now Morbius is using them he has unwittingly conjured up a malevolent force from the power of his own brain, a monster from the id, as it is referred to in the film. Because the monster comes from Morbius's own brain, it is now attacking anyone and everyone who goes against the scientist's wishes.

High spots of the film are the attack of the monster courtesy of an animator on loan from the Disney studios, and a tour of an underground city that is so vast the actors seem antlike in comparison to the huge alien machinery that surrounds them.

The climax of the film comes when Commander Adams, Morbius, Altaira and Robby retreat into the scientist's laboratory, with the monster clawing its way through a sealed door. Morbius eventually realises that the monster is of his own creation and, worried for the safety of his daughter, denies its existence. The monster vanishes, but Morbius is fatally wounded.

In his dying breath, Morbius gives Adams information on how to destroy the Krell machinery and the planet. The survivors escape back to the Commander's flying saucer. Adams and Altaira get ready for a romantic future of their own, Altair-4 explodes and Robby goes on to star in the 1957 science fiction film *The Invisible Boy*.

More than thirty years later, author Stephen King paid homage to *Forbidden Planet* in his book *The Tommyknockers*. In it, people in a small American town start to disappear and one of the characters suggests they might have gone to Altair-4 to picnic among the Krell memory banks.

1957: THE INCREDIBLE SHRINKING MAN

Prolific fantasy, horror and science fiction author and screenplay writer Richard Matheson wrote *The Incredible Shrinking Man* as a novel before adapting it for the screen. The film was directed by Jack Arnold, one of the great science fiction film makers of the 1950s, and starred Grant Williams as hero Robert Scott Carey, better known as Scott.

When a mysterious cloud briefly engulfs a boat on which Scott is sunbathing, he thinks little of it until, six months later, he find his clothes are suddenly too big for him. Scott, for no apparent reason – but in some way connected to the mystery cloud – has begun to shrink.

Despite the fact that he is getting smaller every day, his wife Louise vows to stick by him, but it's difficult due to his mood swings and anger at his situation. When his height gets down to around 3 feet tall, he joins a team of circus midgets who are smaller than him, but soon he is smaller than them as well.

Returning home, he takes to living in a dolls' house, becoming more and more morose at his condition. Things reach a really low point when he is attacked by his own cat, who by now seems like a giant. When wife Louise finds a scrap of Scott's clothing following the attack, she assumes he has been eaten by the cat. But no. He is still shrinking and soon he is doing battle with a comparatively gigantic spider.

The studio bosses at Universal Pictures wanted to give the film a happy ending with doctors discovering a last-minute cure and Scott returning to his proper size. But that was not the way the book ended and director Jack Arnold was determined to be true to the original. By that time, Arnold had won himself a solid reputation with his earlier direction of *Creature from the Black Lagoon* in 1954, along with its successful sequels. So it was agreed that the film with a more downbeat ending could be previewed before a test audience. They gave it their approval and the happy ending was ditched.

As the film ends, Scott has come to terms with eventually shrinking to the size of an atom and no longer fears the future. He has come to realize that to God, there is no zero.

The success of *The Incredible Shrinking Man* was followed by the less successful *The Amazing Colossal Man* in 1957 and, in 1958, by *Attack of the 50 Foot Woman*.

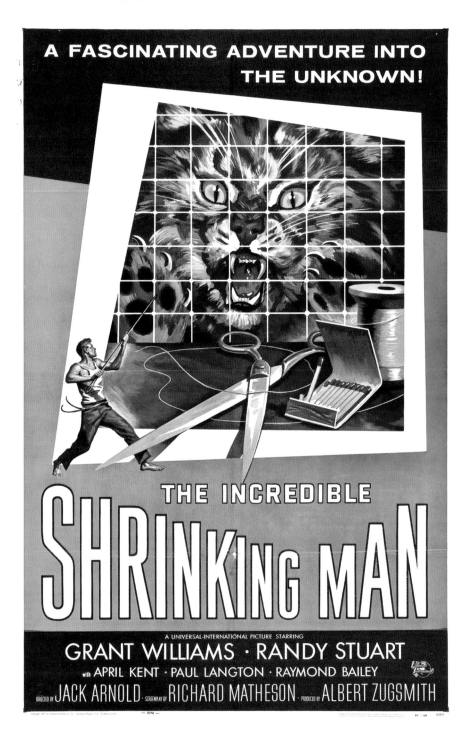

The poster for *The Incredible Shrinking Man*.

1958: THE FLY

The screenplay for *The Fly* was written by novelist, screenwriter and director James Clavell, who later wrote the screenplay for the Second World War movie *The Great Escape*. The film was based on a short story by George Langelaan, a former spy and special agent. It was directed by Kurt Neumann, who came to America during the early days of sound movies and specialised in science fiction films in his later career. It starred David Hedison who, later in his career, played CIA agent Felix Leiter in two James Bond films.

André Delambre is a scientist experimenting with teleportation, a method of transporting matter from one chamber to another using a device called a disintegrator-integrator, a name that really speaks for itself.

Having experimented, not always successfully, on animals, Delambre builds a man-sized chamber and attempts to transport himself. Unfortunately, there is a fly in the chamber with him as he starts the process. When he is disintegrated in the first chamber and then integrated in the second chamber, his and the fly's atoms are mixed up and he ends up with the fly's head and arm, while the fly gets his head and arm. Or, as the film's publicity put it: 'The monster created by atoms gone wild'.

Most of the film is taken up with Delambre's wife Hélène attempting to find the missing fly so that they can reverse the process, while he goes slowly mad. Eventually, she puts him out of his misery by crushing his arm and head in a hydraulic press. She is accused of murder and suspected of insanity. That's when a fly is found caught in a spider's web and it comes as no surprise to find that the fly has a tiny human head and arm. As it hangs there screaming in a tiny, falsetto voice, 'Help me, help me', a spider descends on its prey. Luckily – or unluckily, depending on your viewpoint – there is someone on hand to crush both fly and spider with a rock.

Considering the seeming finality of the ending it might come as a surprise to discover that two sequels were made: *Return of the Fly* in 1959 and *Curse of the Fly* in 1965. The original film was also very effectively remade in 1986.

THE BEST OF THE REST

Monsters, mayhem, flying saucers, aliens and strangely emotionless humans dominated a great many more science fiction films of the 1950s. Here, in brief, are some of the best and worst.

1953: Donovan's Brain

Honest, well-meaning scientists in 1950s science fiction films inevitably get corrupted, and the one in this film, who decides to keep the brain of a ruthless but dead millionaire alive after his death, is no exception. The brain might be in a jar, but it's still capable of exerting its will over the scientist in order to murder old enemies of the now dead millionaire.

1954: Creature from the Black Lagoon

When a geology expedition in the Amazon uncovers a skeletal hand with webbed fingers, it's just the start of their problems. It's not long before a hitherto unknown creature associated with the fossil rises from the swamp and attacks the expedition members. Naturally, a second expedition is set up, which inevitably includes a beautiful and often scantily clad girl. She gets menaced, the expedition members get attacked and the creature is finally shot and sent staggering back to the lagoon from which it emerged.

1954: Them!

The 'them' of the film's title refers to a colony of ants, harmless enough if they had been normal ants, but these specimens are 8 feet long. They are eventually defeated of course, but not before one of the central characters has blamed the mutants on all things atomic. 'When man entered the atomic age he opened the door to a new world,' he comments. 'What we may eventually find in that new world, nobody can predict.' Maybe, but another five years of 1950s science fiction films had a good go at it.

1955: Conquest of Space

Many science fiction films of the 1950s were easy to ridicule; others attempted to tell stories with a little more depth. This was one such. Admittedly, the science is on unsteady ground: a mission to the Moon is changed at the last minute to make Mars the destination. But the film foresees the value of a space station in orbit around the Earth as a launch pad. Also the film deals with religious concepts as a bible-reading crew member begins to question if the mission is right in the eyes of God. In spite of attempts at sabotage, the rocket reaches Mars and, despite snowstorms and earthquakes, eventually makes it into space again for the journey home, when previous disputes among the crew members become reconciled. It was a worthy film, but nowhere near as entertaining as some of the era's more outlandish classics.

1955: The Quatermass Xperiment

The 1953 television serial *The Quatermass Experiment* got the big screen treatment with the title of the film version playing up to the 'X' certificate that it inevitably received. American tough-guy actor Brian Donlevy was somewhat miscast in the role of Professor Quatermass, in place mainly to help sales to the US market. Although based on the original television serial by Nigel Kneale, the screenplay was written by Val Guest, who went on to direct *The Day the Earth Caught Fire*, arguably one of the best science fiction films of all time, even though it escaped the 1950s decade to be released in 1961. *The Quatermass Xperiment* was released in America as *The Creeping Unknown*.

1956: Earth Versus the Flying Saucers

When flying saucers land on Earth, not terribly convincing aliens in metal suits protected by force fields emerge and set out to enslave the human race. But actually it's all a misunderstanding. The aliens really wanted to come in peace, but reacted when they were attacked by humans. For the serious science fiction fan, it's a bit of a letdown to discover the plot is the basic 'We come in peace, shoot to kill' scenario, which was handled so much better in *The Day the Earth Stood Still*. Also disappointing is the fact that the aliens can be killed when they don't have their handy force field with them. So, after the required amount of misunderstanding and bloodshed, they are driven out, and the Earth goes back to normal.

1956: Nineteen Eighty-Four

Two years after the television production of *Nineteen Eighty-Four* caused so much controversy, the film version was less controversial and ultimately less popular with audiences. Straying from the book more than the television adaptation had, it was made more as a typical horror film of its day, epitomised by the poster, which played up the romantic relationship of the two main characters, with the tag line: 'Will ecstasy be a crime in the terrifying world of the future?' Not quite what author George Orwell had in mind when he wrote the original story. Unsurprisingly, the Orwell estate had the film withdrawn from theatrical and television distribution and it can no longer be easily seen.

1957: Quatermass II

American actor Brian Donlevy once again assumed the role of Professor Bernard Quatermass for the film version of the BBC television serial broadcast in 1955. Known as *Enemy from Space* in America, the plot was much the same as that of the television original. This time the screenplay was written by Nigel Kneale, who originated the series for television, and was directed by Val Guest.

1957: The Night the World Exploded

With a title like this and a decade like the 1950s, cinema audiences knew they were in for an hour or so of mindless enjoyment as a new element called E-112 is discovered. It comes from the Earth's core and has an unexpected tendency to explode when exposed to air. Unfortunately, mysterious forces are in action to push piles of E-112 closer and closer to the surface of the Earth. Scientists have only twenty-eight days to find a way to prevent – as the film's title suggests – the Earth exploding.

1958: The Blob

Actor Steve McQueen in one of his earliest film roles, when he could still play a teenager, battles an alien life form that starts out as a small lump of jelly but gradually grows bigger and bigger with each person it meets and devours. The highlight of the film was the gigantic, red blob-like mass of jelly oozing through the projection windows at the back of a cinema to smother and consume the audience. It had more than a few filmgoers glancing anxiously over their shoulders during each performance.

The poster for *The Blob*.

1958: I Married a Monster from Outer Space

The menfolk of the kind of small American town that features as the prime location for so many 1950s science fiction films begin to lose affection for their wives. One of the wives follows her husband when he goes for a walk and discovers he is actually an alien. It turns out that all the women on the alien's planet are extinct, so the males have come to Earth to sire babies with which they can populate their home planet.

1959: Plan 9 from Outer Space

In 1980, a book called *The Golden Turkey Awards*, dedicated to the celebration of low quality films, voted *Plan 9 from Outer Space* the worst movie ever made. Its director Ed Wood also received a Golden Turkey Award for Worst Director. Couple this with the fact that the original title of the film was *Grave Robbers from Outer Space*, and you get some measure of what a good bad film this is. It's the story of alien beings landing their flying saucers in cemeteries to kill grave diggers and resurrect the corpses as zombies. And yet, their intentions are honorable. The plan is to use the zombies to create chaos and prevent mankind from developing a doomsday weapon that could destroy, not just the Earth, but the rest of the Universe too.

The film is a glorious hotchpotch of implausible plotting, amateurish special effects, wooden acting and appalling continuity. It is especially noted for claiming to star old-time horror film actor Bella Lugosi, who was most famous for playing Count Dracula in 1931. Ed Wood had filmed the actor for a different, and soon to be abandoned, project. When Lugosi died, Wood incorporated the footage into *Plan 9 from Outer Space* and claimed him as one of its stars.

1959: Journey to the Centre of the Earth

With the end of the 1950s and the start of the 1960s, special effects in the cinema took a small leap forward. While nowhere near as impressive as the computer-generated imaging that would follow, special effects in 1960s films were definitely in a different league to those of the 1950s. *Journey to the Centre of the Earth* sat right on the cusp between the two eras.

The poster for *Plan 9 From Outer Space*, voted by some as the worst movie ever made.

Based on a Jules Verne novel, written in 1864, the film had a plot that was much more typical of 1950s science fiction, but with the new generation of special effects. As the title dictated, it concerned the adventures of a group of scientists who find a way to reach the centre of the earth, while dealing with deadly rivals, dodging prehistoric monsters who have survived beneath the surface and eventually encountering a subterranean ocean, across which they sail on an improvised raft. Pausing only to explore the sunken city of Atlantis, and fighting off more prehistoric creatures, they eventually make it back to the surface via an erupting volcano.

Journey to the Centre of the Earth made a perfect ending to the 1950s era of science fiction and paved the way for the slightly more realistic stories of the 1960s.

ALL THE FILMS OF THE DECADE

The films detailed so far, both in depth and in brief, only scratch the surface of the great many more made in the 1950s. Some have become classics, others died almost as soon as they were released and, in some cases, even before they managed to get a major cinema release. The following is as near as it can get to a complete list of all the science fiction films, including some that overlapped into the horror genre, that found their way into cinemas from 1950 to 1959.

Abbott and Costello Go to Mars (1953)
Abbott and Costello Meet Dr Jekyll and Mr Hyde (1953)
Abbott and Costello Meet the Invisible Man (1951)
April 1, 2000 (1952)
Attack of the Crab Monsters (1957)
Attack of the 50 Foot Woman (1958)
Attack of the Giant Leeches (1959)
Attack of the Puppet People (1958)
Ballad of the Ming Tombs Reservoir (1959)
Battle Beyond the Sun (1959)
Battle in Outer Space (1959)
Beginning of the End (1957)
Bride of the Monster (1955)

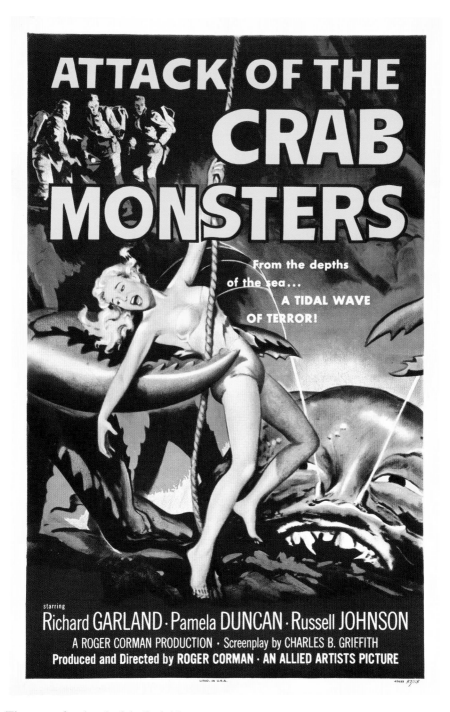

The poster for *Attack of the Crab Monsters*.

Captain Video: Master of the Stratosphere (1951)
Captive Women (1952)
Cat-Women of the Moon (1953)
Commando Cody: Sky Marshal of the Universe (1953)
Conquest of Space (1955)
Crash of Moons (1954)
Creature from the Black Lagoon (1954)
Creature with the Atom Brain (1955)
Day the World Ended (1955)
Destination Moon (1950)
Devil Girl from Mars (1954)
Donovan's Brain (1953)
Earth Versus the Flying Saucers (1956)
Earth Versus the Spider (1958)
Fiend Without a Face (1958)
Fire Maidens from Outer Space (1956)
First Man Into Space (1959)
Five (1951)
Flight to Mars (1951)
Flying Disc Man from Mars (1950)
Forbidden Planet (1956)
4D Man (1959)
Four Sided Triangle (1953)
Frankenstein 1970 (1958)
Frankenstein's Daughter, (1958)
From Hell It Came (1957)
From the Earth to the Moon, (1958)
Giant Gila Monster (1959)
Gigantis the Fire Monster (1959)
Godzilla, King of the Monsters! (1956)
Godzilla Raids Again (1955)
Gog (1954)
Half Human (1957)
Have Rocket, Will Travel (1959)
I Married a Monster from Outer Space (1958)
I'll Never Forget You (1951)

The poster for *Creature from the Black Lagoon*.

Indestructible Man (1956)
Invaders from Mars (1953)
Invasion of the Body Snatchers (1956)
Invasion of the Saucer-Men (1957)
Invisible Invaders (1959)
It Came from Beneath the Sea (1955)
It Came from Outer Space (1953)
It Conquered the World (1956)
It! The Terror from Beyond Space (1958)
Journey to the Centre of the Earth (1959)
Killers from Space (1954)
King Dinosaur (1955)
Kronos (1957)
Lost Continent (1951)
Lost Planet Airmen (1951)
Mesa of Lost Women (1953)
Missile Monsters (1958)
Missile to the Moon (1958)
Monster from Green Hell (1957)
Monster from the Ocean Floor (1954)
Monster on the Campus (1959)
Monster Snowman (1955)
Mysterious Island (1951)
Night of the Blood Beast (1958)
Nineteen Eighty-Four (1956)
Not of This Earth (1957)
On the Beach (1959)
On the Threshold of Space (1956)
Phantom from Space (1953)
Plan 9 from Outer Space (1959)
Port Sinister (1953)
Prehistoric Women (1950)
Project Moonbase (1953)
Quatermass II (1957)
Queen of Outer Space (1958)
Radar Men from the Moon (1952)

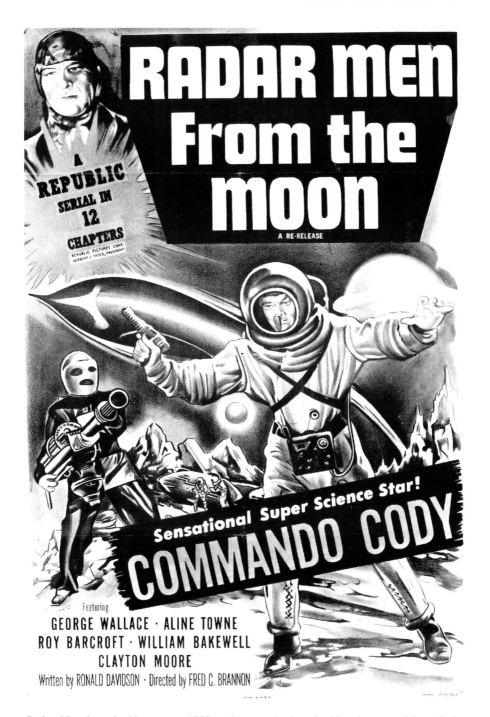

Radar Men from the Moon was a 1952 twelve-part back and white cinema serial, made by Republic Pictures, which ceased movie-making in 1958.

Red Planet Mars (1952)
Return of the Fly (1959)
Revenge of the Creature (1955)
Riders to the Stars (1954)
Robot Monster (1953)
Rocketship X–M (1950)
Rodan (1956)
She Demons (1958)
She Devil (1957)
Snow Creature (1954)
Space Invasion of Lapland (1959)
Space Master X-7 (1958)
Spaceways (1953)
Stranger From Venus (1954)
Superman and the Mole Men (1951)
Tarantula (1955)
Target Earth (1954)
Teenage Cave Man (1958)
Teenage Monster (1958)
Teenagers from Outer Space (1959)
Terror in the Midnight Sun (1959)
The Amazing Colossal Man (1957)
The Angry Red Planet (1959)
The Astounding She-Monster (1957)
The Atomic Submarine (1959)
The Beast from 20,000 Fathoms (1953)
The Beast of Hollow Mountain (1956)
The Beast with a Million Eyes (1955)
The Black Scorpion (1957)
The Black Sleep (1956)
The Blob (1958)
The Brain Eaters (1958)
The Brain from Planet Arous (1957)
The Colossus of New York (1958)
The Cosmic Man (1959)
The Creature Walks Among Us (1956)

The Cyclops (1957)
The Day the Earth Stood Still (1951)
The Day the Sky Exploded (1958)
The Deadly Mantis (1957)
The Electronic Monster (1958)
The Fly (1958)
The Flying Saucer (1950)
The Gamma People (1956)
The Giant Claw (1957)
The H–Man (1958)
The Head (1959)
The Hideous Sun Demon (1959)
The Incredible Shrinking Man (1957)
The Invisible Boy (1957)
The Invisible Monster (1950)
The Jungle (1952)
The Killer Shrews (1959)
The Land Unknown (1957)
The Lost Missile (1958)
The Lost Planet (1953)
The Magnetic Monster (1953)
The Man from Planet X (1951)
The Man in the White Suit (1951)
The Man Who Could Cheat Death (1959)
The Man Who Turned to Stone (1956)
The Manster (1959)
The Mole People (1956)
The Monolith Monsters (1957)
The Monster of Piedras Blancas (1959)
The Monster that Challenged the World (1957)
The Mysterians (1957)
The Neanderthal Man (1953)
The New Invisible Man (1958)
The Night the World Exploded (1957)
The Phantom from 10,000 Leagues (1955)
The Quatermass Xperiment (1955)

The Secret of Two Oceans (1957)
The Space Children (1958)
The Strange World of Planet X (1957)
The Thing from Another World (1951)
The 30 Foot Bride of Candy Rock (1959)
The Trollenberg Terror (1958)
The Twenty-Seventh Day (1957)
The Twonky (1953)
The Unearthly (1957)
The Unknown Terror (1957)
The War of the Worlds (1953)
The Wasp Woman (1959)
The World, The Flesh and the Devil (1959)
Them! (1954)
This Island Earth (1955)
Tobor the Great (1954)
Toward the Unknown (1956)
Twenty Million Miles to Earth (1957)
20,000 Leagues Under the Sea (1954)
Two Lost Worlds (1950)
Unknown World (1951)
Untamed Women (1952)
Varan the Unbelievable (1958)
War of the Colossal Beast (1958)
War of the Satellites (1958)
When Worlds Collide (1951)
World Without End (1956)
X the Unknown (1956)
Zombies of the Stratosphere (1952)

Chapter Four

Science Fiction in Books

'When a day that you happen to know is Wednesday starts off by sounding like Sunday, there is something seriously wrong somewhere.'

Those words more than any others were responsible for my discovery of 1950s science fiction books. They are the opening lines of *The Day of the Triffids*, written in 1951 by John Wyndham. Others may disagree, but for me that was the year that science fiction books came of age. Wyndham's plot might have been fantastic, but he made it believable. It was this, together with subsequent novels by the same author and others of his generation, that were responsible for the genre beginning to be treated with more respect than had hitherto been the case.

Not that science fiction novels hadn't had their share of respectability in the past. It's difficult to identify what was the very first science fiction book, but it is likely to have been *True History*, written in Greek during second century AD by satirist Lucian of Samosata. In it, a group of explorers are blown so far off course they land on the Moon, where they get involved in a war between the inhabitants of the Moon and the armies of the Sun.

Others have argued that a more relevant science fiction first came from Mary Shelley in 1818 when her novel *Frankenstein or The Modern Prometheus* was published. The story of a scientist creating a living creature in his laboratory certainly had all the hallmarks of what would become traditional science fiction, and the novel inspired a new genre of books and plays, not to mention several future generations of films.

In Victorian times there was H.G. Wells churning out his science fiction novels faster than many could read them, starting with *The Time Machine* in 1895 and including classics like *The Island of Doctor Moreau* (1896), *The Invisible Man* (1897*)*, *The War of the Worlds* (1898), *The First Men in the Moon* (1901), and more besides.

A little earlier, in France, Jules Verne was writing his own classic science fiction novels, which, among others, included *From the Earth to the Moon* (1867), *Twenty Thousand Leagues Under the Sea* (1870), *Journey to the Centre of the Earth* (1871) and *All Around the Moon* (1870).

Wells and Verne were both great storytellers, as is witnessed by the number of their books that have lived on in films and other media. Consider H.G. Wells's *The War of the Worlds*, for example. It has been a magazine serial, printed and reprinted in book form countless times, made the basis of a legendary American radio broadcast that was said to have put half of America into a panic in 1938 (not actually true, but the legend endures), been published in comic strip form, filmed in 1953, recorded as a music album by American musician and lyricist Jeff Wayne in 1978 and turned into a blockbusting film starring Tom Cruise in 2005. One can only wonder what old Herbert George would have thought of it all.

Early science fiction novels were treated by readers, unfamiliar with real science, with due respect. But as the world moved into the twentieth century, the genre began to lose ground. This was not because the plots of the stories were in any way less enjoyable than those of their predecessors, but because, as readers became more scientifically knowledgeable, the plots of science fiction books of the time became less believable.

Books such as *Princess of Mars, The Gods of Mars, The Warlords of Mars, Thuvia Maid of Mars* and *The Chessmen of Mars*, all with John Carter as their hero, were written by Tarzan's creator Edgar Rice Burroughs between 1917 and 1922. The plots were entertaining but a long way from scientifically accurate.

That changed in the 1950s as the plots of the decade's novels became more credible, the science more plausible and the stories began to feature the kinds of characters with whom readers could more readily identify. The new wave was epitomised by the aforementioned *The Day of the Triffids*, the book that started science fiction novels in general evolving along a different path. Well, that's my opinion anyway. Feel free to disagree if you wish, but don't ignore the incredible popularity of a great many science fiction books first published in the 1950s and which still remain popular today.

In a book such as this it is impossible to summarise the talents of every science fiction writer of the 1950s. So forgive me if I have missed out your own favourite author or story. What follows is more a personal than a definitive account of the decade's novelists and short story writers.

The War of the Worlds gets the comic book treatment in the August 1927 issue of *Amazing Stories*.

The three giants of the 1950s science fiction book world are usually recognised to be Isaac Asimov, Arthur C. Clarke and Robert Heinlein. Speaking personally, I agree with two of those but would add two more. My quartet comprises John Wyndham, Isaac Asimov, Arthur C. Clarke and Ray Bradbury.

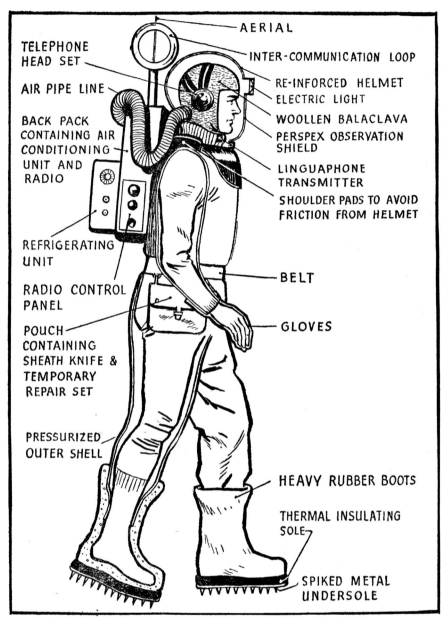

TELEPHONE HEAD SET
AIR PIPE LINE
BACK PACK CONTAINING AIR CONDITIONING UNIT AND RADIO
REFRIGERATING UNIT
RADIO CONTROL PANEL
POUCH CONTAINING SHEATH KNIFE & TEMPORARY REPAIR SET
PRESSURIZED OUTER SHELL

AERIAL
INTER-COMMUNICATION LOOP
RE-INFORCED HELMET
ELECTRIC LIGHT
WOOLLEN BALACLAVA
PERSPEX OBSERVATION SHIELD
LINGUAPHONE TRANSMITTER
SHOULDER PADS TO AVOID FRICTION FROM HELMET
BELT
GLOVES

HEAVY RUBBER BOOTS
THERMAL INSULATING SOLE
SPIKED METAL UNDERSOLE

As 1950s readers became more scientifically knowledgeable, science fiction publications began showing them more of what might be factually possible in the future, as this diagram of a space suit of the future from *Space Story Omnibus* illustrates.

JOHN WYNDHAM

The author who made his name as John Wyndham was born John Wyndham Parkes Lucas Beynon Harris in 1903. Using various pseudonyms, he began selling short stories in 1925, chiefly to the American magazine market. He wrote detective and science fiction stories.

In 1930, he won $100 for the winning entry in a competition to find a suitable slogan for the cover of the American magazine *Air Wonder Stories*. The prize was a generous amount in 1930 and it was no mean feat that his slogan – *Future Flying Fiction*

Author John Wyndham.

– was dreamt up by an Englishman. Unfortunately, the magazine closed soon after.

During the 1930s he wrote mostly under the name John Beynon, with stories that revolved around the anomalies of time travel, interplanetary space exploration, the distant future and even beings who emerged from under the surface of our own planet. His early writing was fantastic, in the true sense of the word, with books that included *Wanderers of Time*, *The Secret People*, *Exiles on Asperus*, *Sleepers of Mars* and *Stowaway to Mars*.

Then, in 1951, all that changed with a book set firmly in the present day and in a part of England familiar to all its readers. With the change of style there came a change of pseudonym. John Beynon became John Wyndham, and the first book he wrote under that name was *The Day of the Triffids*. It set a course for a new style of science fiction stories, often copied but rarely equalled.

John Wyndham died in 1969, by which time, written and published under his various pseudonyms, he had produced an oeuvre of more than twenty science fiction novels and short story collections. His quartet of best-known 1950s classics was *The Day Of The Triffids*, *The Kraken Wakes*, *The Chrysalids* and *The Midwich Cuckoos*.

1951: The Day of the Triffids

The hero of the book is Bill Masen, and the reason why the day he knows to be Wednesday starts off sounding like Sunday is because he is in hospital at the start of the book, with his eyes bandaged. Not being able to see, he listens carefully to the sounds of the hospital and street outside – and everything is far too quiet. The cause, he soon discovers, is that most of the population of Britain, having stayed up late the previous night to watch a mysterious meteor shower, have woken to find themselves blind, and the only reason he has been spared is because his eyes were bandaged during the event.

Masen is a biologist who has been working with triffids, plants that are cultivated for the oil that can be obtained from them. There are, however, three problems with the triffids: they can uproot themselves and move around in a kind of shuffling walk, they seem to be able to communicate with one another and they have a whiplike sting that can lash out to kill, maim or blind anyone who comes too close. None of this is of any consequence, when triffid farmers are on hand to keep control. But with most of the population suddenly blinded, the triffids are free to uproot and go hunting for victims.

It was a triffid sting that put Masen in hospital with damage to his eyes. But since he had been wearing a mask when the plant lashed out at him, only a little of its venom had reached his eyes and no serious harm was done. Once he has removed his bandages, Masen finds he can see well enough. Now it's up to him, and a few others who missed seeing the meteor shower and so retained their sight, to destroy the triffids and rebuild civilisation.

During the course of the book, Masen travels from London to the south of England, meeting on the way Josella Playton, a wealthy novelist with whom he becomes romantically involved. Together they encounter various groups of people who have their own thoughts on how the world should be put back together, not all of them good ideas; a few other sighted people; bands of refugees; a dangerously growing faction out to govern the country and, of course, the rampaging, mobile, sting-lashing triffids.

Much of the book later, he and his followers set up a self-sufficient colony in Sussex, but are forced to flee from the evil forces of the tyrannical new government. Their destination is the Isle of Wight, where they plan to destroy all the triffids on the island and live in peace. There is no happy ending as such, but one day, they resolve, they will return to the mainland to reclaim the country that the triffids have usurped.

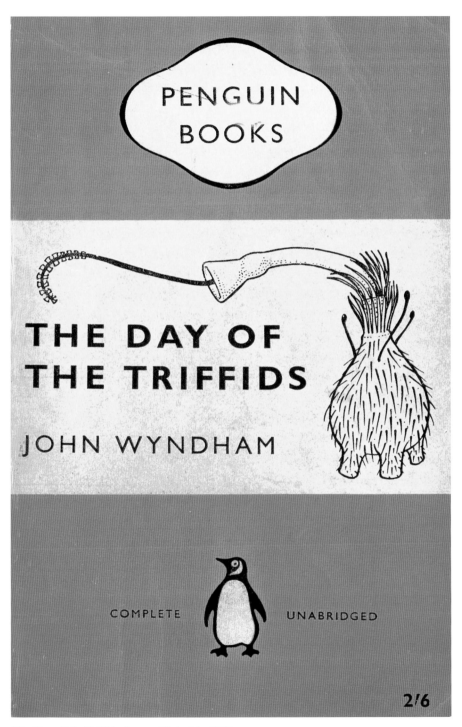

The Day of the Triffids, first published in 1951.

The book was adapted for radio in 1957, 1968 and 2001. A film, set for some reason in France and filmed in Spain, with a plot that wandered some way from the original, was made in 1963. Television serials, whose plots adhered more closely to the book, were broadcast in 1981 and 2009.

1953: The Kraken Wakes

The Kraken of the title comes from a poem by Alfred Lord Tennyson:

> *Below the thunders of the upper deep;*
> *Far, far beneath in the abysmal sea,*
> *His ancient, dreamless, uninvaded sleep*
> *The Kraken sleepeth …*

Equally appropriate to the plot are lines from a nursery rhyme quoted by one of the book's leading characters early on:

> *But Mother, please tell me what can those things be*
> *That crawl up so stealthily out of the sea?*

Attempts to find the origins of this rhyme and its supposed writer, Emily Pettifell, are futile. Both appear to be have been pure fiction, and that in many ways sums up the power of Wyndham's storytelling: everything seems so real and plausible, you assume Emily Pettifell must have been a real person.

As might be guessed from both the fictional and the genuine poetry extracts, this is the story of creatures that emerge from the depths of the sea to sink ships and invade coastal areas. But being a Wyndham story, it's not that simple. Just as the threat from the triffids is increased when most of the population went blind, so the threat from the sea creatures is exacerbated when the polar ice caps begin to melt, and floods proliferate across the globe.

The story is told through the eyes of radio reporter Mike Watson and his wife Phyllis, who, while on their honeymoon cruise, see fire balls falling from the sky and landing in the ocean.

Slowly they, and the rest of the world, begin to realize that the sea creatures are actually aliens who have originated on some planet where

PENGUIN BOOKS

THE KRAKEN WAKES

JOHN WYNDHAM

COMPLETE 2/6 UNABRIDGED

The Kraken Wakes, first published in 1953.

extreme pressures prevail, and therefore are most at home in the depths of the sea, where they build machines to invade the land.

Professor Alastair Blocker, who views the situation with a clearer mind than most, proposes that the two races can live together – us on the land, the aliens in the sea. But, this being a 1950s story, these ideas are never going to be accepted. A bathysphere that is sent to investigate the aliens is destroyed, and naturally the British Government responds by exploding a nuclear bomb at the same location. No wonder the aliens start melting the polar ice caps.

In many ways *The Kraken Wakes* is a political novel written at a time when Britain was still involved in the Cold War between the East and West that followed the Second World War. As the aliens step up their attacks, human opponents, in true Cold War style, refuse to unite against them and begin blaming each other for the developing situation. As a consequence, civilization as we know it collapses and the Watsons, in true Wyndham style, escape a flooded London to live in their holiday cottage in Cornwall, which by now is on its own island in the middle of the rising sea. Here, they are totally isolated, until a neighbour arrives in a rowing boat to tell them that the world has been saved.

Luckily, the Japanese have developed an underwater ultrasonic weapon to kill the aliens. The reader is left wondering how the world will survive now that its population has been reduced to a fraction of its original size, new landmasses have been created and the planet's climate has been permanently changed.

But, as Phyllis points out in the final pages, in prehistoric times there had been a great plain covered in forests, and then the water had arrived and drowned it all, which created the North Sea. 'I think we've been here before,' she says, 'and we got through it last time …'

1955: The Chrysalids

When he was young, David Storm sometimes dreamt about a city that would be perfectly familiar to the average reader. It was on the coast, with tall buildings around a harbour full of boats and cars travelling along the roads. It is, however, unfamiliar to young David who lives in a close-knit commune where no building is taller than one or two storeys, horsepower

PENGUIN BOOKS

THE CHRYSALIDS

This thrilling and
realistic account of a
world beset by genetic
mutations is a worthy
successor to
The Day of the Triffids
The Kraken Wakes
'Much charm and impressive
technical skill'
STAR

JOHN WYNDHAM

2/6

The Chrysalids, first published in 1955.

is the only means of transport and he has never seen the sea, let alone a boat.

This is a post-apocalyptic era following some kind of tragedy that has decimated the human race. Nuclear war is never mentioned as such, but it is intimated, even though the people of the settlement where the story begins have their own account of what happened. In their twisted version of history, there were the Old People who were technologically advanced but died out when God sent the Tribulation to destroy them.

The beliefs they have developed are based on keeping their race pure of mutations, which are thought to be the work of the Devil. Mutations range from crops that stray from the norm, to deformed animals and even humans, all of which must be rooted out and destroyed. Which is unfortunate for David's friend, a young girl called Sophie who has six toes. To make matters worse, David is the son of the community's religious leader. To further complicate things, David and some of the other children are telepathic, in particular David's cousin Petra who, despite being very young, has a more powerful form of telepathy than any of the others. All of which must be kept from the grown-ups, who would see them as mutants.

When Petra's telepathy is under threat of being discovered, a group of telepathic children flee the community, travelling into the Fringes, a lawless area full of mutations and other contaminated badlands. The characters in the book might not be aware of it, but it becomes obvious to the reader that these are areas contaminated by radiation and nuclear fallout.

After several adventures, pursuits, captures and escapes, Petra makes telepathic contact with a community in a distant country called Sealand that survived to live a normal life, but which to David and his friends sounds totally alien. Avoiding a posse of people determined to capture them and bring them to justice, David and some – though not all – of his friends are rescued by the people from Sealand, who have followed Petra's psychic signal to find them. The journey, of course, ends in the city that David has been dreaming of all his life.

1957: The Midwich Cuckoos

On a night one September, a strange fog envelopes the very English village of Midwich, rendering its inhabitants unconscious. The next morning the

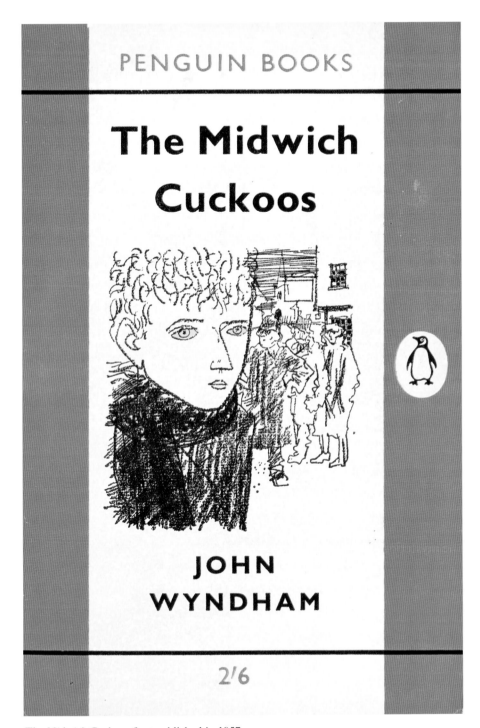

PENGUIN BOOKS

The Midwich Cuckoos

JOHN WYNDHAM

2'6

The Midwich Cuckoos, first published in 1957.

fog clears, the villagers wake up seemingly perfectly healthy and with no side effects. That is, until all the women of childbearing age discover they are pregnant. After an appropriate time, thirty-one boys and thirty girls are born. They all look perfectly normal, apart from their golden eyes.

The narrator of the story is Richard Gayford, a writer who, with his wife, was absent from the village on the night of the mass impregnation. He watches as the children grow up at a faster rate than is normal, and it soon becomes apparent that they possess a form of group mind control that they can use to protect themselves. If any of them is hurt, the perpetrator ends up dying at his own hand in some way.

It comes to light that other communities of similar children have been born in other countries around the world. The other groups, however, have all been destroyed by various means initiated by those around them who had discovered their powers early.

The Midwich children do everything in their power to defend themselves and they demand aeroplanes from the government to take them to a secure location where they can live and grow together. The authorities think this a bad idea, but are helpless to do anything about it. They can't separate the children, and simply bombing the village would destroy the civilian population as well as the children.

The day is saved by an academic in the village called Gordon Zellaby. He has been mentoring the children and he is the one person they trust more than any other. But Zellaby has a terminal illness, so has nothing to lose when he smuggles a bomb into the place where they are all living. Fighting their attempts to get into his mind and discover his plans, he manages to detonate the bomb, killing himself in the process, while ridding the world of the mysterious and malevolent Midwich cuckoos.

BEST OF THE REST

Among the many other successful books and short story collections written by John Wyndham, the following six are generally accepted as the best:

1956: The Seeds of Time

A collection of ten short stories, dealing with time travel, space exploration and other more down-to-earth plots, some of which are surprisingly poignant from an author not known for his sentimentality.

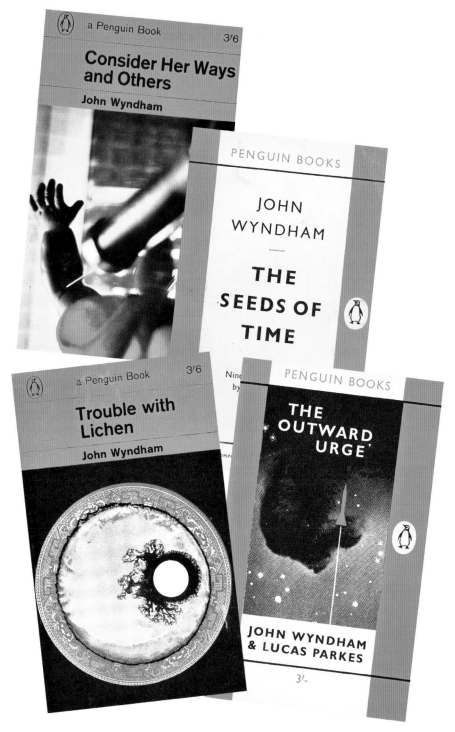

A selection of other science fiction novels and short story collections written by John Wyndham.

1959: The Outward Urge

Four stories about four generations of a family involved with building the first space station, plus landings on the Moon, Mars and Venus. The book was supposedly written with Lucas Parkes as technical adviser. Mr Parkes, we now know, was another of Mr Wyndham's several pseudonyms.

1960: Trouble with Lichen

The story of the problems that arise after the discovery of antigerone – a drug that raises life expectancy to up to 300 years.

1961: Consider Her Ways and Others

A collection of six short stories whose title story is about a woman who partakes in an experimental drug programme and wakes up in the future. Other story plots in the collection include time paradoxes, demons and parallel universes.

1962: Jizzle

A collection of fifteen short stories kicking off with a monkey artist out for revenge, a woman who meets her future self, an underground train that takes its passengers straight to hell ... and other plots that could be conceived only by John Wyndham.

1968: Chocky

The story of a young boy who has an imaginary friend who turns out to be much more than something from his imagination.

ISAAC ASIMOV

Isaac Asimov was one of the 1950s authors who put the science into science fiction. His novels and short stories were rarely fanciful, and much more concerned with the possibilities of what might be scientifically authentic. Whether he was dealing with interplanetary travel, robots or time travel, the reader was always left with the feeling that what happened in his stories, while not actually possible in the preset day, would probably be achievable sometime in the future. And the fact that his regular column in *The Magazine of Fantasy and Science Fiction* each month dealt with factual science, gave veracity to the most fantastic of his story plots.

Asimov was born in Russia in 1920, but was brought to America in 1923 and become a US citizen in 1928. His father owned a confectionary shop that also sold magazines, which is where he first became acquainted with science fiction. His early life, however, was more involved with science fact. Majoring in chemistry, he gained an undergraduate degree from Columbia University

Author Isaac Asimov in the 1950s.

in 1939 before moving on to take his MA in 1941 and PhD in 1948. The following year he took on the role of Associate Professor of Biochemistry at Boston University School of Medicine.

Although Asimov didn't leave academia to become a full-time writer until 1958, he began his quest to become a science fiction writer much earlier. His first published story, *Marooned off Vesta*, appeared in *Amazing Stories* magazine in 1939. Like many of his contemporaries he soon developed an association with John W. Campbell Junior, the legendary editor of *Astounding Science Fiction* magazine, who was famous for nurturing fledgling writers to develop ideas and generally mature in their fields. There followed several years of success with Campbell's magazine.

During the 1950s, and with many published short stories to his name, Asimov embarked on two mammoth series of books that would dominate his writing and the science fiction book world throughout the decade. They became known as the *Foundation* and the *Robot* books.

1951: Foundation

Set in the far future, *Foundation* is the story of the Julactic Empire, comprising more than a million worlds throughout the Milky Way. As the book begins, times are changing. The Empire has been around too long and is starting to descend into barbarism. Enter Hari Seldon, a mathematician who can use mathematics to foresee the future – and what he sees is the Empire descending into 30,000 years of anarchy. Getting together with a team of psychologists, artisans and engineers, he sets out to create a new Empire to be called the Foundation, a force that would be dedicated to art, science and technologies doomed to be lost forever if the Empire deteriorated in the way his prophesies indicated.

The way forward, according to Seldon, is to create an Encyclopedia Galactica, which would include the sum total of all human knowledge. It is agreed by those who rule the Empire that Seldon and his team be allowed to instigate this work, providing they do so while in exile on a remote planet called Terminus. Terms are agreed, but Seldon also sets up a second Foundation in a secret location.

Fifty years later, with Seldon now dead, the work continues, but is hampered by interference from other planets that surround Terminus. But then a vault is opened that reveals a hologram of Seldon explaining what his true purpose had been. It turns out to be little to do with the establishment of the Encyclopedia and more to do with getting the people he wanted settled on Terminus to put into play various actions that his mathematical calculations had shown would come to pass.

There will, it seems, be a series of crises in the years ahead, which will be overcome and, in so doing, will help reduce the dark ages ahead from 30,000 years down to a mere thousand. Seldon's hologram also reminds the people of Terminus that there is a Second Foundation at the opposite end of the galaxy. Then the hologram fades away, leaving the people of Terminus to work things out for themselves.

There follows a series of political manoeuvres in which the mayor of Terminus plays various planets against one another in order to leave the Foundation untouched, before being overthrown by another politician who succeeds in bringing more planets into the Foundation's domain. It's clear that the Foundation is growing and will soon be a threat to the old Empire.

Foundation, first published in 1951.

Foundation and Empire, first published in 1952.

1952: Foundation and Empire

As book two in the trilogy begins, the Foundation and the Empire are squaring up for a battle for supremacy. When a general in the Empire's hierarchy launches an attack on the Foundation, the Emperor, suspicious of his general's motives, cancels it. The Foundation becomes the victor. The event, though not the outcome, was foreseen by Seldon, whose hologram appears again and explains the clash between the two powers was inevitable and good for the Foundation whichever side won. A weak attack would have shown the enemy up for its weakness; a strong attack would have alerted the Emperor to a threat to his position.

One hundred years goes past, then a new threat emerges in the form of a mutant called The Mule who begins to take over and conquer Foundation planets, by way of psychic suggestions to their inhabitants. It prompts loyal Foundation people to begin looking for the location of the Second Foundation, previously mentioned by Seldon, in the hope that its people can help fight The Mule.

Then it all gets even more complicated. One of the characters discovers the location of the Second Foundation, but is killed before it can be revealed. Then it turns out that The Mule has been using his powers to drive the search, so that he can find the Second Foundation for himself. When his ruse is exposed, he retreats, but his search for the Second Foundation continues.

1953: Second Foundation

Part three of the *Foundation* series is divided into two parts. In the first, the reader is shown how The Mule tries to find the Second Foundation, intent on its destruction. Unfortunately the people of the Second Foundation, although in an unknown location, manage to telepathically modify The Mule's brain so that he loses interest in them. So he retires to rule over his previously conquered planets, and little more is heard of him.

The second part of the book deals with the First Foundation's search for the Second Foundation. It does so by producing a device that jams telepathic abilities, while causing pain to telepaths. Knowing that the people of the Second Foundation are telepathic, this leads them to the Second Foundation, which turns out to be on the same planet as the First Foundation.

Second Foundation, first published in 1953.

Seldon had originally described the Second Foundation as being at the other end of the galaxy from the First Foundation, but the galaxy is not disc-shaped, but shaped like a double spiral, meaning the two ends are actually quite close.

Having located fifty telepaths, the First Foundation destroys them in the mistaken belief that it has now destroyed the Second Foundation. There is, of course, a lot more to the book than this brief outline. But suffice to say that, as the book ends, all is not as it seems …

Foundation follow-ups

It was author Douglas Adams who, after writing what was originally meant to be only three books in the *Hitchhiker's Guide to the Galaxy* series, added another to what became referred to as a trilogy in four parts. Then, when yet another book was written, it was described as the fifth book in the increasingly inaccurately named Hitchhiker's Trilogy. It was a line of thinking that might equally be applied to Isaac Asimov's *Foundation* books, written as a trilogy in the 1950s and considerably expanded upon in the 1980s and 1990s.

In 1986, the author published *Foundation's Edge*, which continued the search for the Second Foundation, by which time the inhabitants of the various planets involved have actually forgotten about the existence of a mythical planet called Earth. In *Foundation and Earth*, published in 1986, the search for Earth takes centre stage.

After furthering the initial story in the first two new novels, Asimov then went back in time and wrote a couple of prequels. In *Prelude to Foundation*, published in 1988, Hari Seldon is once more very much alive and being forced into exile. In *Forward the Foundation*, published in 1993, Seldon is working out his mathematical theories, which were at the heart of the original trilogy, and puts a plan into action to set up the Second Foundation, ahead of the First Foundation.

For Asimov fans, these last two books are more than just prequels; they are more like a kind of time travel in which the reader gets to see the cause of an effect that has already been witnessed.

During the time that Asimov was writing the *Foundation* books, he was also involved in writing several other interlinked series of novels and short stories, and in the latter books he began to tie together stories from one series to another. This was most notable in the *Robot* books that began life in the 1950s.

Asimov's Robot books

Unlike the Foundation series, the *Robot* books were not written as episodes of a single cohesive story. They comprised thirty-eight short stories and five novels written from 1920 to 1992. At the start of the 1950s, he began to weave the stories together.

I, Robot, published in 1950, was a collection of nine short stories that had been published previously, but which were now put into a single volume. The central theme was an interview with a twenty-first-century psychologist who specialises in studying artificial intelligence, and ways of solving the problems that can be caused by intelligent machines. The book was the inspiration for the film of the same name made in 2004.

I, Robot was followed by *The Caves of Steel* in 1953 and *The Naked Sun* in 1955. They concern an earthman called Elijah Baley, a plainclothes homicide detective in a far future version of the New York City Police Force. Elijah has an assistant called R. Daneel Olivaw. Despite his resemblance to a human, the 'R' in his name stands for robot. Together, the human and robot team face conflicts between the people of a much-overcrowded Earth and others known as Spacers, the descendants of humans who settled on other planets many years before.

Essentially, both novels are far future versions of the traditional detective story. In *The Caves of Steel*, the human and robotic detectives investigate the murder of a Spacer ambassador who lives in an area for his kind outside New York City. In *The Naked Sun* the detective duo investigates another murder, this time that of a foetal scientist who runs a birthing centre on a Spacer planet named Solaria.

Asimov continued to write his *Robot* stories for many years after the end of the 1950s, completing the quartet of novels with *The Robots of Dawn* in 1983 and *Robots and Empire* in 1985.

The *Robot* series is particularly famous for Asimov's Three Laws of Robotics, which are first introduced in *I, Robot* and run, not only through his own stories, but find their way into several other non-Asimov stories.

The most notable example is Robby the Robot in the 1956 film *Forbidden Planet*, who finds it impossible to harm any human. The three laws are these:

1. A robot may not injure a human being or, through inaction, allow a human being to come to harm.
2. A robot must obey orders given to it by human beings except where such orders would conflict with the First Law.
3. A robot must protect its own existence as long as such protection does not conflict with the First or Second Law.

Asimov's other books

Isaac Asimov was a prolific writer who wrote and edited an almost unbelievably huge number of books for both adults and children, with a new book, and sometimes more than a single volume, published nearly every year throughout his writing life. Other than the *Foundation* and *Robot* books, and ignoring his enormous outpouring of work after the 1950s, the books published in that decade alone included:

1950: Pebble in the Sky
1951: The Stars Like Dust
1952: David Starr, Space Ranger
1952: The Currents of Space
1953: Lucky Starr and the Pirates of the Asteroids
1954: Lucky Starr and the Oceans of Venus
1955: The End of Eternity
1956: Lucky Starr and the Big Sun of Mercury
1957: Lucky Starr and the Moons of Jupiter
1958: Lucky Starr and the Rings of Saturn
1958: The Death Dealers
1955: The Martian Way
1957: The Earth is Room Enough
1959: Nine Tomorrows: Tales of the Near Future

Asimov also wrote books and magazine articles on general science, mathematics, astronomy, earth sciences, chemistry, biochemistry, physics, biology, history, the Bible, literature, humour and satire, as well as producing four autobiographies.

Isaac Asimov continued writing and editing books until his death, aged seventy-two, in 1992.

ARTHUR C. CLARKE

Arthur Charles Clarke was an English science fiction writer born in 1917. His first job was with the Treasury Department of the British Government, where he worked as an auditor. During the Second World War he served as a radar instructor with the Royal Air Force, leaving the forces in 1948 to take a Bachelor of Science degree at King's College, London. From 1946 to 1947, and then again from 1950 to 1953, he was Chairman of the British Interplanetary Society. Founded in 1933 and still in existence today, the Society is known for the ways in which it promotes the exploration and use of space for the good of humanity.

Prince Claus of the Netherlands (left) presents Arthur C. Clarke with the Marconi International Fellowship Award in 1982.

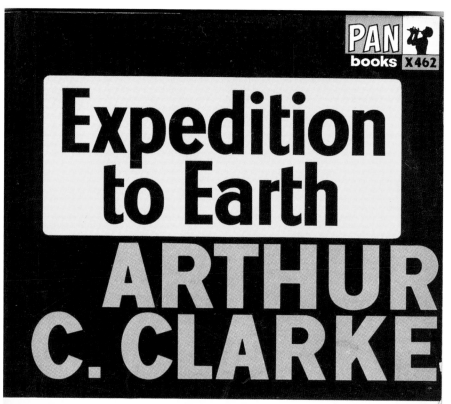

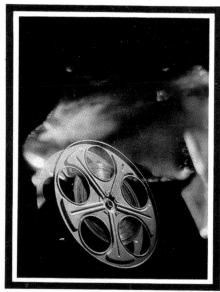

Expedition to Earth, first published in 1953.

During most of this time, however, like so many of his contemporaries, Clarke was involving himself with science fiction and writing short stories. He sold his first two stories to the American *Astounding Science Fiction* magazine in 1946. The first to sell was called *Rescue Party*, which appeared in the May issue of that year, but the first to be published was the second sale, *Loophole*, which had appeared the previous month. His early stories often centred on a single scientific fact, which led to the basic premise of the story, and then to a twist ending of some kind.

Clarke's first book, *Prelude to Space*, was written in 1947 and appeared as a novel in *Galaxy* magazine in 1951, the same year as his second novel, *The Sands of Mars*, was published in book form. *Prelude to Space* went on to be published as a book in 1953.

Although known for his novels, many of Clarke's short stories have, since their publication, become classics, most notably one called *The Sentinel*, which was largely responsible for changing his career. Clarke wrote the story in 1948 for a BBC writing competition, but it failed to win a place. It was, however, subsequently published in a magazine called *Ten Story Fantasy* in 1951 before appearing as one of a collection of stories in the 1953 anthology *Expedition to Earth*. The story concerns the discovery of a strange artefact on the surface of the Moon, which has been built by an alien race millions of years before. It transpires that it was most likely left there as a warning beacon to the people of Earth when they reached the space age.

The Sentinel is often quoted as being the story on which film director Stanley Kubrick based his 1968 film *2001: A Space Odyssey*. This is not entirely true. The story undoubtedly inspired the film, but the fusion of many new ideas brought in as Clarke and Kubrick together wrote the screenplay made the film very different from the story. It can be said, however, that the story was the starting point for the film, and its plot introduced a new, more esoteric voice to much of the author's work.

Arthur C. Clarke died, aged ninety, in 2008, having lived since 1956 in Sri Lanka. He was knighted for his services to literature in 2000. Many of his more famous – and some have argued his best – short stories and novels were written in the 1960s and 1970s. But the 1950s still saw the publication of three notable works that cannot go unmentioned: *The Sands of Mars*, *Childhood's End* and *Earthlight*.

1951: The Sands of Mars

This was the book that began Clarke's career as a well-respected science fiction novelist. Although a previous novel and many short stories had already appeared in science fiction magazines, *The Sands of Mars* was the author's first novel to be published as a book.

Published in 1951, ten years before Yuri Gagarin became the first man in space, eighteen years before Neil Armstrong became the first man to walk on the Moon and who knows how many years ahead of who might one day become the first man to land on Mars, the book is an early indication of the way Clarke's storytelling would develop. The science is a mixture of what was possible in 1951, alongside extrapolations of what Clarke clearly thought would be possible in the future.

The hero of the story is Martin Gibson, a science fiction writer who is a guest on a flight to the Red Planet where a colony has already been established. Unlike a lot of contemporary science fiction, the rocket he and the crew travel on does not take off from Earth, but from an orbiting space station (again, written twenty years before, in the real world, a space station was even launched).

As a writer, and during the course of the journey, Gibson asks questions about the technology of space flight, which again brings science fact – or what one day might be fact – to the readers of the 1950s.

Once on Mars, Gibson is allowed to move around freely, meeting the people who run the already established base, getting tangled up in a dust storm and even meeting a form of semi-intelligent life. This latter was perhaps the one thing that Clarke got wrong scientifically, but it should not be forgotten, that among all this science fact, this is a science fiction novel.

Gibson discovers that plants are being cultivated to enrich the planet's oxygen, and that the scientists on Mars are working towards exploding Phobos, one of the Martian moons, to turn it into a new sun that would orbit the planet. The theory is that this would bring heat to help nurture the oxygen-giving plants, with the result that Mars might one day have a breathable atmosphere.

At the end of the book, Gibson decides to stay on in the colony as a kind of public relations man in charge of publicity to help encourage Earth people to colonise the planet.

The Sands of Mars was a perfect first novel for Clarke, setting the tone for the kind of scientifically plausible science fiction he would write in the years

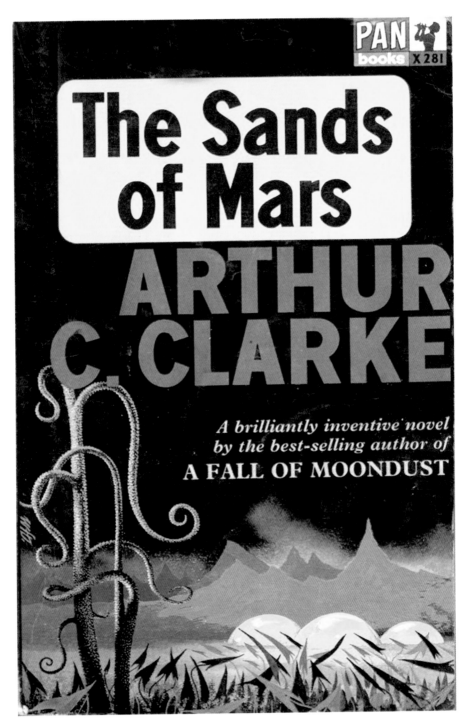

The Sands of Mars, first published in 1951.

ahead. It illustrated his ability to foresee what kinds of scientific discoveries might be on the horizon and to make them seem entirely possible in the years he was writing.

1953: Childhood's End

What many believe to have been Clarke's best novel began life as a short story called *Guardian Angel*, written in 1946. It concerns an alien invasion by a race who become known as the Overlords. At first sight, the aliens seem to be entirely peaceful. In fact they impose total peace on Earth by preventing anyone waging war or generally acting in a harmful way to one another. Their leader, Karellen, assumes supervision of all human affairs in order, he says, to prevent the human race becoming extinct. The Overlords also introduce amazing new technologies to the people of Earth.

The world enters a new Golden Age, even though the Overlords don't reveal themselves to the people of Earth for fifty years. When they do, Earth people are in for a shock because the Overlords resemble ancient ideas of what the Devil looked like. Nevertheless, most of Earth acquiesces to the rule of their alien masters. There are, however, those who rebel, claiming that Earth has lost its desire to advance and innovate.

Then, sixty years after the Overlords first made contact, strange things begin to happen. Children are born who go on to develop psychic and telekinetic powers. What soon becomes apparent is the real reason why the Overlords have made contact and remained overseeing Earthly affairs.

It transpires that the Overlords serve an enormous cosmic intelligence called the Overmind, which comprises an amalgamation of many ancient civilisations and without any form of material existence. The Overlords cannot join the Overmind, but they can act as intermediaries, introducing new civilisations to it, ready to be amalgamated. That's what the new generation of Earth children is being bred for. As the minds of the psychic children meld into one, they cease to be individuals and transform into a single mass consciousness, which is assimilated into the Overmind.

When the Overlords leave, mankind is bereft. No more children are born and – in the way that much of 1950s science fiction came to dictate – it becomes the end of civilisation as the last straggling people of Earth might once have known it.

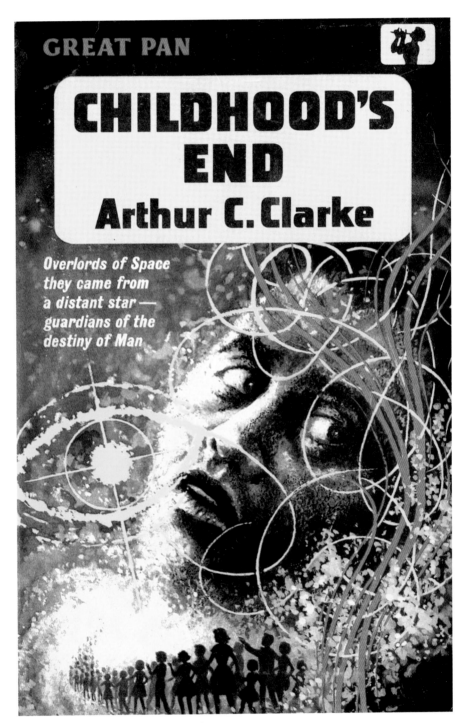

Childhood's End, first published in 1953.

1955: Earthlight

Some science fiction authors of the 1950s wrote books whose plots, when examined carefully, were little more than variations on the same theme. Not so Arthur C. Clarke. Having dealt in his first two novels with the colonisation of Mars and the destruction of Earth, he turned his attention, with this third book, to interplanetary politics.

As the book opens, Earth is politically united with a single government. Elsewhere, settlers have made homes on other planets in the solar system. What unites the settlers and the Earth government is the need on both sides for certain heavy metals. When it emerges that such metals might be found on the Moon, and that the government of Earth aims to monopolise them, warfare erupts.

The main plot hinges on the exploits of Bertram Sadler who goes undercover to the Moon's observatory to seek out the spy who has been transmitting information about the Moon's metals and the intentions of the Earth government to the interplanetary settlers.

As the two sides battle it out, Clarke introduces the kinds of ideas that only he could write about with the kind of authority that makes them believable: a revolutionary kind of spacedrive for the Settlers and a weapon that fires electro-magnetically propelled liquid metal for the Earth people.

War is waged between the two sides, space cruisers are destroyed, daring rescue missions take place as a third cruiser threatens to explode in a nuclear blast and, in the end, the fight between Earth and the colonists reaches no definitive conclusion. It seems that Sadler is doomed to not even unearth the spy.

Many years go by before the memoirs of one of the battle's commanders reveals that the information came from a member of the observatory staff whom Sadler had met when he was first sent to the Moon. The novel finishes with the revelation of a piece of technology that enabled the spy to transmit his information from the Moon to the settlers. He simply placed an ultraviolet source at the point in the observatory's telescope where light rays from far objects converge. In this way he was able to transmit his messages over many millions of miles of space.

Once more, Clarke takes impossible technology and makes it all seem perfectly feasible.

Earthlight, first published in 1955.

After the 1950s

As the 1950s ended, Clarke's stature as a science fiction novelist of tremendous perception steadily grew. These are just some of the better-known and more remarkable novels that followed.

1961: A Fall of Moondust

The story of a tourist vessel that sinks into the dust of a lunar crater and the efforts taken to rescue the passengers.

1963: Glide Path

A non-science fiction novel dealing with the development of a ground-controlled aircraft landing system, inspired by Clarke's years as a radar instructor in the Royal Air Force.

1968: 2001: A Space Odyssey

Developed from the plot of the film of the same name, written by Clarke and the film's director Stanley Kubrick. Clarke followed the original story with new ones of his own in *2010: Odyssey Two*, *2061: Odyssey Three* and *3001: The Final Odyssey* in 1982, 1987 and 1997 respectively.

1973: Rendezvous with Rama

The interception by human explorers of a cylindrical starship that enters the Earth's solar system and the discovery of a complete world on the inside cylindrical surface of the ship. Clarke followed up the book with *Rama II*, *The Garden of Rama* and *Rama Revealed* in 1989, 1991 and 1993 respectively.

1975: Imperial Earth

An account of one man's journey to Earth from his home world of Titan in 2276 to celebrate the 500th anniversary of the American Independence.

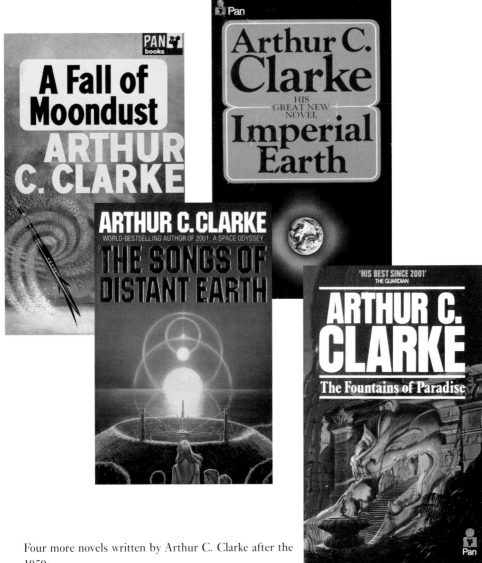

Four more novels written by Arthur C. Clarke after the 1950s.

1979: The Fountains of Paradise

The story of a space elevator travelling on a super-strength strand of wire from the ground to an orbiting satellite more than 20,000 miles above the Earth.

1986: The Songs of Distant Earth

The effects on a peaceful colony of humans whose ancestors long ago came from Earth, and who know little today about their home world, when their planet is visited by a ship from Earth on its way to the stars.

Clarke also wrote hundreds of short stories and published anthologies of them throughout his career. In his later years he wrote in association with fellow authors and science fiction enthusiasts who included Gentry Lee and Stephen Baxter.

RAY BRADBURY

Ray Douglas Bradbury was born in 1920. From an early age he determined to be a writer and by the time he left school he was sending regular stories to markets such as *The Saturday Evening Post*, today a bimonthly American magazine but which, in the 1950s, was published weekly. None succeeded in selling.

Eventually he came to a decision. If he had not sold a story by the time he was twenty-one, he would give up. In 1941, a few months before the date in question, Bradbury sold a story, co-written with fellow science fiction fan and writer Henry Hasse. The story was called *Pendulum* and it appeared in *Super Science Stories* magazine.

Author Ray Bradbury, photographed in 1975.

Spurred on by his success, Bradbury wrote fifty-two more stories, one a week, for the next year. He made three sales.

Although the author has a few good novels to his name, he was best known for his short stories, some of which stood alone, others of which were inter-connected by a single idea or theme. One such collection of stories became his first book, published in 1947 and called *Dark Carnival*. A few years before that, however, in 1944, he had begun to collect together a series of stories about the colonisation of Mars, which would eventually become a book that was somewhere between an anthology of short stories and an episodic novel. It was published in America as *The Martian Chronicles* in 1950 and, in 1951 in Britain, as *The Silver Locusts*.

During the 1950s Bradbury flirted for a short while with the movies. In 1952, film director and screenplay writer John Huston, most famous in the 1940s for his films *The Maltese Falcon* and *The Treasure of the Sierra Madre* and, in 1951, for *The African Queen*, contacted Bradbury with a proposal to turn *The Martian Chronicles* into a film. That production never came to fruition but the contact paved the way for the author to write the screenplay for Huston's 1956 film of *Moby Dick*. The experience was not a happy one, with Bradbury having to continually defend his writing to Huston, who had his own ideas of how the screenplay should be written. It probably didn't help matters that Huston was more used to writing his own screenplays and Bradbury admitting from the outset that he had never been able to read the original novel by Herman Melville.

In 1953, two of Bradbury's short stories were turned into films, neither of which bore much resemblance to the originals. The films were *It Came from Outer Space*, based on a short story called *The Meteor*, and *The Beast From 20,000 Fathoms*, based on a story called *The Foghorn*.

Awards won for his work included the 2000 National Book Foundation Medal for Distinguished Contribution to American Letters, the 2004 National Medal of Arts and the 2007 Pulitzer Prize Special Citation.

Ray Bradbury died in 2012, aged ninety-one. Most of the books he left behind were collections of short stories. His anthologies of stories published in the 1950s included *The Illustrated Man*, *The Golden Apples of the Sun*, *The October Country*, *A Medicine for Melancholy* and *The Day It Rained Forever*. His three best works of the 1950s were *The Martian Chronicles*, *Fahrenheit 451* and *Dandelion Wine*.

1950: The Martian Chronicles

The stories that make up *The Martian Chronicles* and which tie the overall narrative together were, at the time of their publication, unlike anything seen before. Bradbury has often been criticised for knowing too little about science

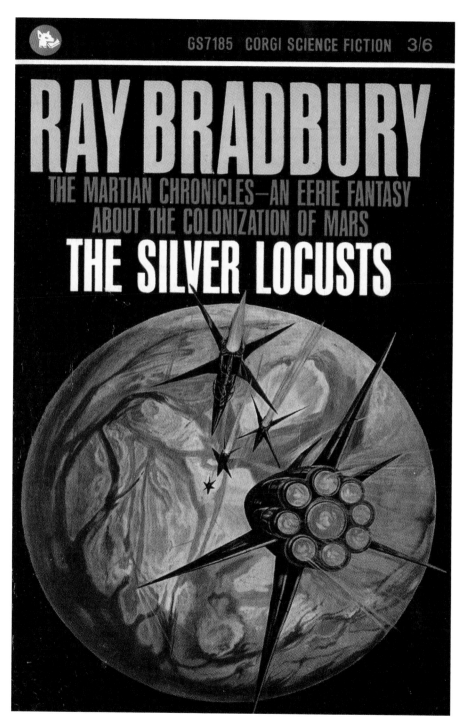

GS7185 CORGI SCIENCE FICTION 3/6

RAY BRADBURY

THE MARTIAN CHRONICLES—AN EERIE FANTASY ABOUT THE COLONIZATION OF MARS

THE SILVER LOCUSTS

The Martian Chronicles, also known as *The Silver Locusts*, first published in 1950.

to write decent science fiction and nowhere is this better illustrated than in his Martian stories. But in the end, it doesn't matter, because the stories transcend the criticisms. Bradbury's Mars has a breathable atmosphere. Martians exist and live in houses of crystal pillars that turn flowerlike to face the sun. The canals of the Red Planet are full of water. The Martians travel across deserts in sand ships. The science is all wrong, but the stories are superb.

The individual stories are tied together by a plot that concerns people from Earth setting out to colonise Mars, how their first few attempts are thwarted by the gentle, peace-loving but slightly sinister Martians, and how the Earth people eventually conquer all. It's a story that draws parallels with the way Native Americans were ousted by early immigrants to America, or how Australia and New Zealand were colonised at the expense of native Aborigine and Maori cultures.

Yet the stories, even when they involve prejudice and violence, are still told in a poetic manner that is unique to Bradbury's writing style. It was the book that established him early in his career as one of America's foremost new writing talents.

When, in 1951, the book was published in England as *The Silver Locusts* (a reference to the rockets that took the people to Mars and the way they swarmed across the planet), writer and critic Angus Wilson said of it: 'For those who care about the future of fiction in the English language, this book is, I believe, one of the most hopeful signs of the last twenty years.' The satirical magazine *Punch* added: 'To take the paraphernalia of science fiction – the rocket ships, the robots and galactic explorations – and fashion from them stories as delicate as Cezanne's watercolours is a very considerable achievement. It is hard to speak with restraint of these extraordinary tales.'

1953: Fahrenheit 451

The title of what was Bradbury's first true novel, as opposed to interlinked short stories, was taken from the temperature at which book paper is reputed to catch fire and burn. The story is set in the future when firemen are employed not to put out fires but to start them, to burn books and the houses of anyone found in possession of them.

The hero is a fireman named Guy Montag who, at the start, believes that all books are evil. His views are slowly changed by his neighbour, a

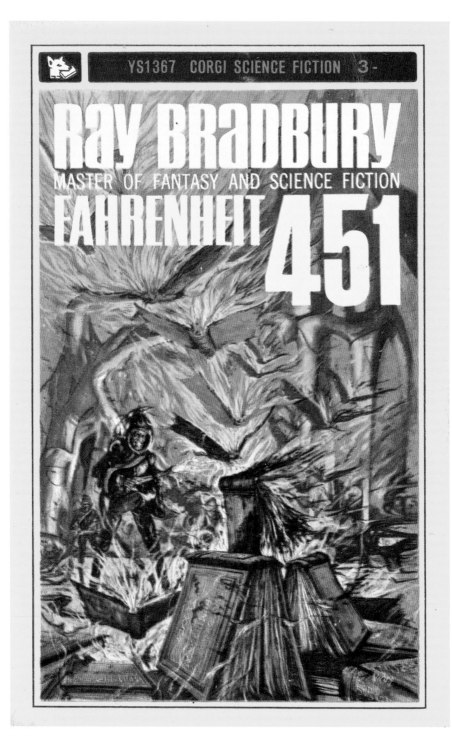

Fahrenheit 451, first published in 1953.

A 1960 edition of *The Magazine of Fantasy and Science Fiction*, which featured the short story *Bright Phoenix*, which inspired *Fahrenheit 451*.

young woman called Clarisse, who has a very different lifestyle to his own. Gradually she begins to show him that there is more to life than he has supposed.

Later, when attending a fire that is planned to destroy a house and the book collection of an old lady, he steals a book and reads it in secret. Gradually he comes to realise his way of life is wrong, and how everyone around him has become ignorant of anything and everything other than watching banal interactive television programmes.

As he begins collecting more books, the inevitable happens. He is found out and, as a fireman, is forced to burn his own house. Before he can be taken captive for his book reading crimes, he escapes and eventually finds his way to a group of drifters and exiled book lovers. Each one has memorised a book of their choosing, so that if society is ever rebuilt, the books, passed on by word of mouth though generations, will be available again.

Fahrenheit 451 was filmed in 1966 by the French director François Truffaut. Since it concerned the abolition of the written word, all the film's opening credits, which would normally have been written, were spoken over a series of colour-filtered pictures of television aerials. The final scenes of the book, featuring people in a snowy forest walking among the trees, each reciting aloud the words of the book he or she has memorised, were particularly poignant.

Fahrenheit 451 started as a short story, *Bright Phoenix*, written and rejected by several markets in 1947–48. In 1951, a version of the story, now titled *The Fireman*, was published in *Galaxy Science Fiction* magazine. Long after the literary success of the book was assured, *Bright Phoenix* appeared in the September 1960 British edition of *The Magazine of Fantasy and Science Fiction*.

1957: Dandelion Wine

Strictly speaking, this book does not belong here because it is not science fiction, even though it does have elements of fantasy to it. 'The haunting novel of a summer of terror and wonder,' was how the publishers described an early edition of the book. Despite it being a different genre, for those interested in Bradbury's work as a whole, it is not to be missed.

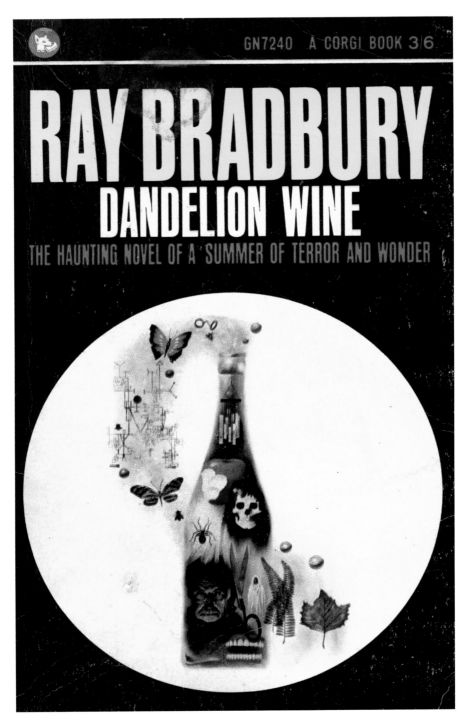

GN7240   A CORGI BOOK 3/6

RAY BRADBURY
DANDELION WINE
THE HAUNTING NOVEL OF A SUMMER OF TERROR AND WONDER

Dandelion Wine, first published in 1957.

Like other Bradbury books, *Dandelion Wine* is really a collection of short stories, previously published in various magazines, woven together with a simple narrative, in this case that of a young boy growing up during the course of a single summer.

The boy is Douglas Spalding, and it's likely to have been no coincidence that Douglas was Ray Bradbury's middle name, because the stories are based very much on the author's own experiences of growing up in a small town in

A selection of some of Ray Bradbury's work published after the 1950s.

Illinois. The dandelion wine of the title is made by Douglas's grandfather. Throughout the book, it stands as a kind of allegory for the joys of summer and how they can be experienced by the young.

It's not science fiction, but it overlaps at times into the kind fantasies that science fiction readers enjoy, all written in Bradbury's inimitable prose. 'Dandelion wine,' says the young Douglas at one point in the book. 'The words were summer on the tongue. The wine was summer caught and stoppered.'

In 1971, Apollo 15 astronauts named an impact crater on the Moon Dandelion Crater in honour of the Bradbury book.

Bradbury after 1959

Ray Bradbury rose to fame in the 1950s, but much of his finest work was published in the 1960s, through to the 1990s. The best of his later novels and short story anthologies included *Something Wicked This Way Comes*, *The Halloween Tree*, *Death is a Lonely Business*, *A Graveyard For Lunatics*, *Green Shadows White Whale*, *From The Dust Returned*, *Let's All Kill Constance* and *Farewell Summer*.

The short stories that were published in magazines, collected in more Bradbury books and amassed with the stories of other authors in anthologies make a massive oeuvre of work far too large to mention in detail here.

OTHER SCIENCE FCTION WRITERS OF THE 1950s

The four authors covered above were by no means the only science fiction writers at the height of their powers in the 1950s. Among others prominent in the field were the following.

Robert Heinlein (1907–88): Heinlein is thought by many to have been the greatest of all science fiction writers of this decade and he is often referred to as 'the dean of science fiction'. He was one of the authors who truly brought respectability to the genre with a series of novels and stories that fell mainly into the hard science fiction category. Among his more famous 1950s books were *The Green Hills of Earth*, *Farmer in the Sky*, *Between Planets*, *The Rolling Stones*, *The Star Beast*, *Tunnel in the Sky*, *Double Star*, *Time for*

The Green Hills of Earth, by Robert Heinlein, first published in 1951.

the Stars, Citizen of the Galaxy, The Door into Summer, Have Space Suit – Will Travel, Methuselah's Children* and *Starship Troopers.* He continued to produce a prodigious number of novels and short stories well into the late 1980s.

Brian Aldiss (1925–2017): Brian Aldiss was an English writer of novels and short stories who was said to have been influenced greatly by the writing of H.G. Wells. In 2000, he was named Grand Master by The Science Fiction Writers of America. In the 1950s, Aldiss's books included *The Brightfount Diaries, Space Time and Nathaniel, Non-Stop, The Canopy of Time* and *No Time Like Tomorrow.*

A.E. Van Voigt (1912–2000): Born in Canada, Alfred Elton Van Voigt wrote books often regarded as complex and a little mysterious, with interlocking plots full of surprises and shocks. His 1950s work included *The House That Stood Still, The Voyage of the Space Beagle, The Weapon Shops of Isher, The Mixed Men, The Universe Maker, The Mind Cage* and *Empire of the Atom.*

Clifford D. Simack (1904–88): Simack was a newspaperman by trade, who was employed full time in the newspaper business from 1939, working part-time as a science fiction writer of short stories and novels. He became a full-time writer only on retirement. His 1950s body of work included *Time and Again, City* and *Ring Around the Sun,* and he was prolific in both novel and short story writing until the late 1980s.

Eric Frank Russell (1905–78): Although English and living in England, Russell found science fiction fame in America as one of the first Englishmen to become a regular contributor to the American *Astounding Science Fiction* magazine, the like of which was not prevalent in Britain at the time the writer began his career. His first story, called *The Saga of Pelican West,* appeared in the magazine as early as 1937. His books in the 1950s included *Sentinels from Space, Three to Conquer, Wasp* and *The Space Willies.* Despite being English, he wrote in a very American style.

Philip K. Dick (1928–82): More than twenty years after the 1950s ended, Philip K. Dick won fame as the author of a novel and a short story on which

Three to Conquer, by Eric Frank Russell, first published in 1957.

two iconic movies were based. The 1982 film *Blade Runner* was based on Dick's 1968 short story *Do Androids Dream of Electric Sheep?* The 1990 film *Total Recall* was based on the author's 1966 novel *We Can Remember It For You Wholesale.* Overall he wrote forty-four novels and 121 short stories. Included in nearly twenty novels of the 1950s were *Gather Yourselves Together*, *Voices from the Street*, *Dr Futurity*, *The Cosmic Puppets*, *Solar Lottery*, *Eye in the Sky*, *The World Jones Made*, *The Broken Bubble* and *Time Out of Joint.*

Among a great many other science fiction writers who were active in the 1950s were Alfred Bester, James Blish, Bertram Chandler, John Christopher, L. Sprague de Camp, Frederik Pohl, C.M. Kornbluth, Theodore Sturgeon, Algis Budrys, Zenna Henderson, E.E. Doc Smith … and many more.

Chapter Five

Science Fiction Comics and Magazines

In the 1950s a comic was generally aimed at young children with the stories told in pictures, either by text beneath each picture or by the use of speech balloons. Most, though not all, were printed on cheap newsprint type of paper. Magazines were more sophisticated, some aimed at older children, but most published for young and more mature adults. They were glossy, printed on better paper and with colour covers, even if, in those days, most of the content inside was still in black and white. At least that was largely the case in Britain. In America, there were magazines and comics that matched the British types, but there was also more of a crossover between the two, with comic books that took the format of magazines, but with pages of stories, some of which were told in a comic strip, speech balloon style.

In Britain, it was sometimes possible to find science fiction comic strips in national newspapers or in some children's books and annuals, but by and large, at least in the early 1950s, comics and magazines specifically dedicated to science fiction were thin on the ground. America, with its comic book culture, was where the action was, and had been for some years previously. Among the different kinds of publication in America at that time there were the slicks and the pulps. The slicks were glossy, upmarket magazines that used two or three short stories in each issue, some of which might have been science fiction. The pulps were generally regarded as coming from the other end of the market, where they resided with other specialist magazines and comic books produced on cheap paper with garish covers and packed full of short stories. Both types were printed in, or close to, what was known as the octavo size of 6 x 9 inches. Many American science fiction magazines of the time also favoured the smaller, digest size of approximately 5½ x 7¾ inches.

Science fiction was far from the only genre covered by the pulps. Other subjects included horror and terror. In fact there were two pulps called *Horror Stories* and *Terror Tales*. Then there were the detective story magazines where a number of science fiction writers, like John Wyndham,

Rex Strong Space Ace, a rare British comic strip that appeared with science fact and fiction articles and stories in the1955 book *Space Story Omnibus*.

cut their teeth. They had titles like *Inside Detective*, *Confidential Detective*, *Front Page Detective*, *Official Police Detective* and many more of a similar ilk. Alongside these there were the more notorious pulps with names like *Man*, *Men*, *Man's Life*, *Man's Illustrated*, *Real Men* and *Men Today*. The majority of these, whatever the subject matter inside the magazine, had one thing in common: lurid covers, which inevitably showed beautiful women in various states of undress having nasty things done to them. Depending on the subject matter of the publication, the perpetrators included sadistic criminals in the detective pulps; cruel Nazis (remember the Second World War had only be over a few years at this time) in the men's pulps; and monsters, mad scientists or aliens in the science fiction pulps.

Running a close second to the way the stories were illustrated on the covers of most magazines was the way they were described on the contents pages. Here are three of my favourites.

Journey's End by Walter Kubilius: Through space they plunged for a dozen lifetimes, on a journey which had yet to begin. – *Super Science Stories*

The Dancing Girl of Ganymede by Leigh Brackett: She was like a dream come to life, with hair of tawny gold and the glowing face of a smiling angel. But she was not human! – *Thrilling Wonder Stories*

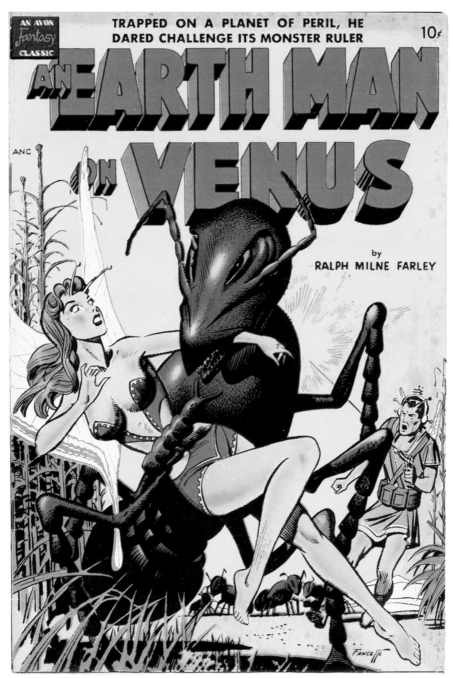

American science fiction pulps like this Avon Fantasy Classic with its women in peril theme did little to persuade doubting parents that their children really only wanted to read about rocket ships and robots.

Rampart of Fear by Benjamin Ferris: Panic-stricken he fled from the wrath of men to face the mindless clutching tendrils of the alien hunger-things that demanded his life, for the life they fed! – *Super Sciences Stories*

When American magazines like these began to appear in Britain in the 1950s, they were all branded as horror comics by the more reserved Brits who had not encountered anything like them before. This was bad news for kids like me who could not understand why, when asking parents or grandparents to buy them totally innocuous children's comics like *Beano* or *Dandy*, would be mystified about why they were cross-examined to make sure the title in question was not 'one of those horror comics'.

Unfortunately, 1950s American science fiction magazines, most of which were equally guilty of decorating their covers with women in peril, got lumped in with all the rest. Despite the fact that they might contain stories from eminent science fiction authors, they remained high on the banned list for adults monitoring and attempting to censor their children's reading habits.

For the budding science fiction aficionado of the 1950s, however, all was not lost. Around the middle of the decade Superman and Superboy arrived in two different comic books, closely followed by Batman and Robin in their own. No lurid covers, no women in peril, just superheroes going about their business.

OMNIBUSES

An omnibus, in literary rather than transportation terms, was a book, the size usually similar to children's comic annuals, but with content associated more with science fiction monthly magazines and weekly comics. Hence their inclusion in this chapter, rather than the one dedicated entirely to books. Several such British omnibuses were published in the 1950s.

Space Story Omnibus

Space Story Omnibus was produced by the English publisher Collins in 1955, and so popular that it was reprinted a year later. The book contained nine short stories by Edward Boyd, a popular writer of the day, all with good

Space Story Omnibus was designed like a book, but with contents more usually found in science fiction magazines and comics.

pulp fiction titles like *Space Pirate*, *A Matter of Time*, *Mutiny in Space* and *The Miraculous Mushrooms*. Intermingled with the stories were science fact articles on subjects like space exploration, space medicine and space stations. These articles, along with the storyline for comic strips epitomised by *Rex*

Return to Earth: artwork by Bruce Gaffron for *Space Story Omnibus.*

Strong, *Space Ace*, were supplied by technical writer Maurice Allward. Throughout, the book was illustrated with black and white line drawings and remarkably perceptive full-page colour plates showing the future that space travel could have in store, including the building of a space station and how rockets might return to Earth. Of the several artists whose talents were

An illustration by Len Fullerton, drawing under the pseudonym Nat Brand, for a story called *Operation Mirror*, which appeared in both *Space Story Omnibus* and *Whopper Space Stories*.

showcased in the book, the foremost was Bruce Gaffron, who left the UK to live and work in America in the 1950s. He died in California in 2011. Other artwork from the book came from Len Fullerton, a well-respected nature and wildlife artist, who used the pseudonym Nat Brand for his science fiction comic book illustrations. He died in 1968.

Some of the stories, articles and artwork contained in the pages of *Space Story Omnibus* went on to be included in other omnibuses with names like *Whopper Space Stories* (1959) and *The Giant Book of Amazing Stories* (1960).

THE COMICS

Aimed mostly at young children, British comics rarely published science fiction stories. There were, however, a couple of notable exceptions. One was the massively popular and well-respected *Eagle*; the other, rather unexpectedly, was *The Dandy*.

Eagle

The first issue of *Eagle* appeared on 14 April 1950 and immediately sold out 900,000 copies. Within a short while sales passed the million mark. It wasn't surprising considering the sheer quality of the publication, which put it head and shoulders above the majority of most traditional children's comics of the time. The printing, the paper, the intricacy of the artwork and the amount of colour were all vastly superior to its rivals – and all for fourpence halfpenny (or 4½d – less than 2p in today's decimal coinage). It was an impressive debut, but getting to publication had been a long and arduous process.

Eagle was the brainchild of Marcus Morris, Vicar of St James's in Birkdale, Lancashire. Soon after his appointment he transformed the local parish magazine into a publication designed to be a place where issues could be hammered out. Hence its name: *The Anvil*. It was that publication that formed the starting point for *Eagle*, whose name, it is thought, was derived from the eagle on a lectern in Morris's church.

Morris was aware of the rise in popularity of American comics, professionally produced but with content that he considered often violent and obscene. His aim was to provide a comic that was entertaining for the young, while at the same time providing some kind of moral guidance. He

Marcus Morris inspecting artwork for *Eagle*.

was soon joined in his quest by a young artist from the local art school. His name was Frank Hampson and he became enthused with Morris's idea for a comic character called Lex Christian whose exploits would be exciting, but with a strong moral undertone. The original concept was to produce a comic strip for a national newspaper, but it wasn't long before that idea was abandoned in favour of producing an entirely new type of children's comic.

Bringing others on board and in the face of mounting debts, the team began work early in 1949 and worked continuously until April 1950. With debts mounting by the day and against setbacks from potential publishers, some of whom showed no interest in the new comic, others who showed mild interest before backing away, Morris battled to find someone to publish his comic. Eventually, after a great many disappointments, the project was taken on by Hulton Press, publishers of *Lilliput* and *Picture Post*, two very popular magazines of the day.

The badge that was still proudly worn by members of the Eagle Club in the 1970s.

At its peak, *Eagle* had 200 staff who worked eight-hour shifts, twenty-four hours a day, seven days a week. The comic also ran the Eagle Club, whose members received a badge, a rulebook and a list of privileges. Within months of its launch, the club boasted 100,000 members, who were sometimes targeted by Hulton with questionnaires about the comic and ways in which it could be improved.

Dan Dare

Lex Christian, who had started off as a parson in the London slums, turned into a flying padre who, in the early comics, was depicted as Chaplain Dan Dare of the Inter-Planet Patrol, wearing a traditional chaplain's dog collar. Before long, however, Chaplain Dare was transformed into *Eagle's* most popular character of all time: Dan Dare, Pilot of the Future.

Although Dan Dare's adventures were set in the late twentieth century, the characters were reminiscent in many ways of the stiff upper lip heroes of Second World War films and stories. The main characters lined up like this.

A bust of Dan Dare on exhibition at The Atkinson Museum in Southport.

Dan Dare appeared on the first and second page of every issue of *Eagle*.

Daniel McGregor Dare was a man with a great sense of honour, known for always keeping his word. Violence was never his first reaction to a situation and, whenever possible, he would use intelligent peaceful ways out of the many predicaments in which he found himself. He worked for the Interplanetary Space Fleet as the organisation's chief and extremely skilled pilot.

Albert Fitzwilliam Digby, better known simply as Digby, was Dan Dare's batman. He was at Dan's side through every story, somewhat bumbling but always loyal.

Sir Hubert Guest, whose cartoon character was based on Hampson's father, was the Controller of Space Fleet. A veteran pilot, he remained mostly grounded, but occasionally joined Dan on some of his missions.

Professor Jocelyn Mabel Peabody was the strip's only female character, known for dreaming up many of the ideas that got Dan into and out of trouble.

The Mekon, Dan Dare's worst but most popular enemy, was perhaps the most notorious of all the comic strip's characters. He was a Venusian with an overlarge green head and small body, known for the way he transported himself around on a saucer-shaped flying boat. He commanded the Treens, an army of large, green-skinned, reptile-like soldiers, all of whom were devoid of emotions.

Sondar was a reformed Treen, who became loyal to Space Fleet and accompanied Dan on many of his adventures.

Frank Hampson was the genius behind the creation of Dan Dare. The comic strip might have evolved without him, but it would not have been the same, and it is doubtful that it would have been as successful. Hampson not only drew the comic strip, he also conceived many of the stories. He was a man dedicated to his art, working to the point of exhaustion to render his characters and their surroundings in painstaking detail. He often used real people as models for his drawings and as ways of capturing accurate facial expressions.

Hampson's attention to detail in his drawings was astonishing. Backing up the actual strips published in *Eagle* and which were the only drawings his readership ever saw, was a wealth of annotated drawings and concept artwork, mostly drawn by Hampson himself, but some of which were drawn and annotated by other artists in the *Eagle* studio. These drawings showed

Surrounded by schoolboy readers, Frank Hampson, the creator of Dan Dare and whose work contributed so much to the success of *Eagle*.

everything from the details in Dan Dare's spacesuit to vehicles driven by the Treens and other characters. The tent in which Sondar lived was, for example, annotated in full detail in one drawing, despite the fact that it only made a fleeting appearance in a couple of frames of the published strip. In another drawing, many of Digby's personal details and effects were shown, right down to a menu of his favourite food, its contents clearly changed and adapted by the artist until he was satisfied with the result.

Eric Eden was one such artist. He had studied at the Southport School of Art with Hampson, then worked with him during the early years of *Eagle* before leaving after objecting to the long hours that the job entailed and then rejoining in 1955. Eden was particularly adept at working up technical plans and details of hardware to which Hampson could refer when producing the final artwork for a *Dan Dare* strip.

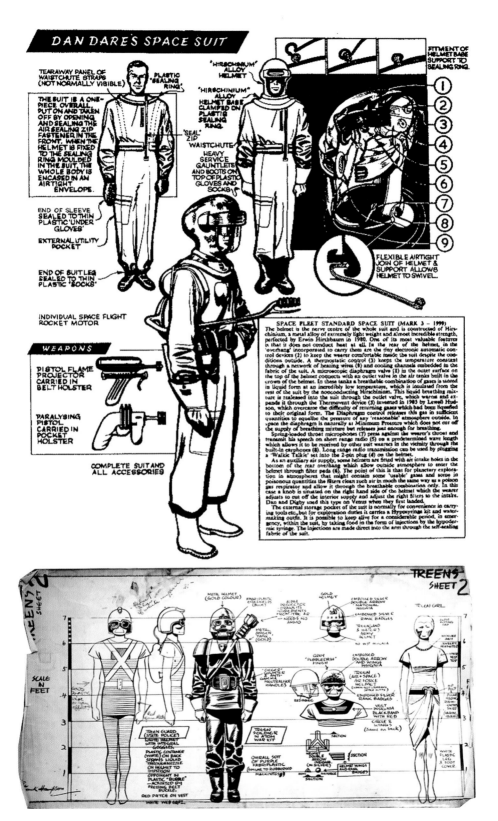

Preliminary annotated drawings by Frank Hampson show the meticulous detail the artist applied to his characters, in this case the clothing worn by Dan Dare and the Treens.

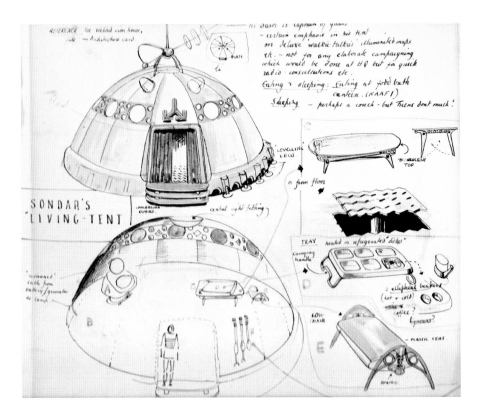

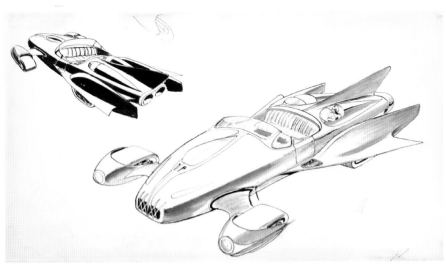

Thought to be the work of artist Eric Eden and one other unknown artist from the *Eagle* art studios, these reference sheets from around 1957, shown here and on the following pages, are concept sketches that refer to characters, vehicles, kit and hardware to be later incorporated into a Dan Dare adventure called *Reign of the Robots*.

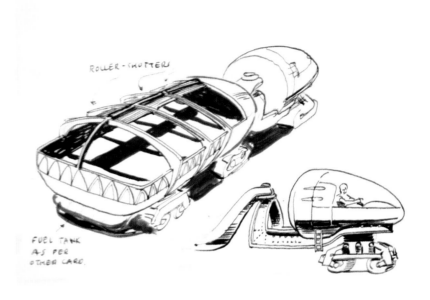

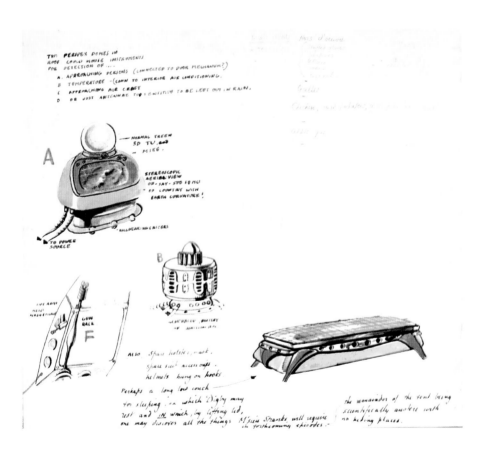

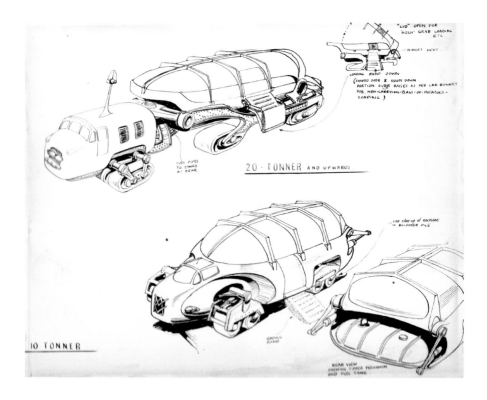

None of these drawings, by Hampson, Eden, or any other *Eagle* artist, ever saw publication. They were prepared simply as detailed references to ensure maintenance of continuity in characters, places, vehicles and a lot more besides in the finished drawings.

Dan Dare's first outing was in a story called *Voyage to Venus*. It concerned Dan and his faithful crew making a trip to Venus to find new resources that would help an overpopulated and starving Earth. Unfortunately, on arrival, they find Venus is populated and ruled over by The Mekon, who is in the throes of planning the conquest of Earth. Only Dan's stiff upper lip can save the world.

At the end of creating the first serial, Morris, afraid of losing readers, took out a full-page advertisement in *Picture Post*, telling readers that Dan Dare's adventures with The Mekon and Treens on Venus might have ended, but more adventure awaited him on Mars. The advertisement was illustrated by Hampson to show Dan Dare standing heroically in front of his spaceship, ready for action.

J.H.Hamilton Esq
Keeper
Mappin Art Gallery
Weston Park
Sheffield
S10 2TP   9th August 1978

Dear Mr.Hamilton

Thank you for your letter. I would certainly be prepared for
you to have my Mekon for exhibition, especially as you intend
showing Frank Hampson originals. I worked closely with Frank
in the Mekon's development and he has the original prototype
head that I made. I too have a collection of Hampson originals
mostly unpublished ideas for characters such as the Mekon.

I must add, however, that the Mekon I enclose suffered
severe damage in transit to Italy recently and another is
under construction from the mould. All things being equal
I should have another completed well within time for your
exhibition.

He measures 3 feet from the top of his dome to seat. The
boat is 3 feet 6 inches long and 20 inches wide and stands
on a 4 foot plinth.

                              Yours sincerely

                              Pip Warwick

A letter from Pip Warwick to the Keeper of the Sheffield Mappin Art Gallery describes his sculpture, mentioning that the first Mekon has been damaged and that another is under construction.

Morris needn't have worried about losing his schoolboy readers. They remained loyal to *Eagle* and Dan Dare until the last issue of the comic in April 1969, by which time Hampson was no longer involved in the artwork.

Such was the enduring interest in Dan Dare in general and The Mekon in particular, that a life-size model was created in the 1970s by Pip Warwick, a figurative ceramic sculptor and lecturer at Newcastle University. He was a fan of Dan Dare, having grown up reading *Eagle* in the 1950s. Much of

Sculptor Pip Warwick at work on his life-size sculpture of The Mekon.

his work revolved around contemporary myths, which led him to approach Frank Hampson about the creation of a Mekon ceramic sculpture. Hampson gave his blessing and Warwick began working on prototypes of the alien's head, followed by a full-size ceramic version of The Mekon travelling on his

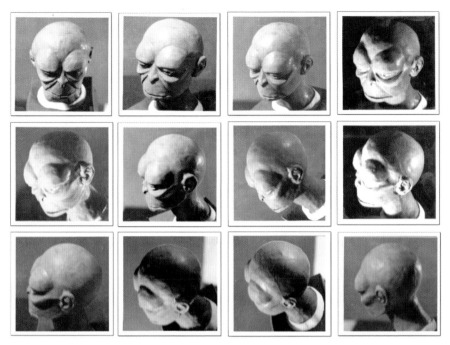

Pip Warwick's prototype of the ceramic Mekon's head.

One of Pip Warwick's finished ceramic sculptures of The Mekon.

A 1954 advertisement that encouraged readers to buy Dan Dare products.

space boat. In a 1978 letter to the Keeper of Sheffield's Mappin Art Gallery, where Warwick's Mekon was due to be exhibited, the sculptor describes it as measuring 3 feet from his dome to his seat, with the alien's flying boat measuring 3 feet 6 inches long and 20 inches wide, standing on plinth that measured 4 feet.

Eagle was relaunched under a new publisher in March 1982, complete with the adventures of Dan Dare's grandson and the return of The Mekon. But the new stories never captured the imagination of a generation in quite the same way as those in the original comic with its famous 1950s science fiction hero.

Back in the 1950s, although Dan Dare led the way with science fiction stories in *Eagle*, Frank Hampson's comic strip hero wasn't alone in the pages of the comic.

Professor Puff

David Langdon was a largely self-taught artist whose day job was working in the Architects Department of London County Council. In his spare time,

Professor Puff, a children's science fiction strip that appeared in *Eagle*.

however, he was a cartoonist whose first work was published in the Council's journal, *London Town*. From there, he went on to successfully contribute cartoons to *Punch*, the well-known satirical magazine, and he published a book of his cartoons in 1941.

In 1953, Langdon began drawing a children's science fiction cartoon for *Eagle*. It was called *Professor Puff and his Dog Wuff*. A far cry from the colourful and intricately drawn artwork of Hampson's Dan Dare, Langdon's drawings were sparse and printed only in black and white. They concerned the simple and somewhat childish adventures of an eccentric professor, who wears a business suit and space helmet, and his dog, also wearing a space helmet, who get caught up with aliens, flying saucers and various forms of space travel mayhem.

Advertisements

Even some of the advertisements in *Eagle* took on science fiction themes. In the 1950s, Coleman's mustard ran a regular series of quarter-page advertisements in the form of a serial about *The Three Mustardeers* who, in one series, travelled in a time ship to partake of various adventures with aliens on an asteroid in the year 2154.

THE THREE MUSTARDEERS " IN THE FOURTH DIMENSION "

CHAPTER 7

KROOL

(RECAP: *The Three Mustardeers, travelling with Professor Lumb in his Time-Ship, reach the year 2154, and land on the asteroid Ceres. The Professor is captured by " blue men ", but the Mustardeers escape to a city, and climb a high building. Roger and Jim reach the roof. But Mary hangs precariously, her fingers slipping.*)

Roger scrambled along the narrow back of the gargoyle towards Mary. The beam of a paralysing light swung towards him. And on the roof, Jim suddenly shouted :
" Roger ! Look out below!"

One of the " blue men " raised a short weapon like a blunderbuss, and fired. A small round glass object whistled past Mary and burst on the wall behind her, emitting a cloud of yellow gas. At the same moment, Mary screamed; her fingers lost their grip; Roger lunged forward and grabbed her by the wrist; while Jim threw himself flat on the roof and seized Roger's ankle.

Jim heaved at Roger. Roger hauled at Mary. And soon all three were safe—coughing and choking as the gas swirled round them.

Roger dragged Mary to her feet. " It's poison gas," he spluttered. " Come on, quick!"

With the boys helping Mary, they escaped across the City, leaping effortlessly from roof to roof—against the tiny gravity-pull of Ceres.

They soon out-distanced their pursuers on the ground, and at last halted at the side of the city nearest to the Spaceport. They were on the roof of a large ornately decorated structure—obviously the principal building of the city. In the middle was a domed transparent skylight. Glancing down through this, Jim gave a sudden shout:
" Gosh ! . . . Roger ! Mary ! Come here quick !"

Below them was a vast hall, like the state room of a barbarian palace. Groups of " blue men " stood beside a raised throne, on which sat a " blue man " of enormous height, wearing

a crimson cloak and horned headdress of gold. And kneeling before the throne, guarded by four armed " blue men ", was the hapless Professor.

Beside Roger was an electrical locking device with a switch. Roger pressed it. Half of the dome slid noiselessly open, and voices came up to them clearly from the hall below.

The man on the throne was speaking—and, to the amazement of the Mustardeers, was speaking English.

" Your story of a Time-Ship," he said to the Professor, " is a futile lie. This is the Earth-Year 2154, and you are a spy from Earth."

The Professor started to protest, but the guards silenced him.

" Blow it!" Jim said. " We've got here too late. I wonder what's been happening to the Prof."

" Quiet!" said Roger. " Listen!"

The man on the throne rose to his feet, pointed at the Professor, and spoke again:—
" I, Krool, Chief of Ceres, condemn you to immediate execution as a spy. Remove him!"

The guards seized the struggling Professor, and marched him towards the exit from the hall, while the Mustardeers looked on in silent horror.

(Next part—" The Spaceship " on August 6.)

A Coleman's mustard advertisement from 1954 featuring a science fiction trio called The Three Mustardeers.

The Dandy

The Dandy Comic, as it was originally known, was first published in 1937. It was aimed at young children and rose to fame as one of the first comics to use speech balloons rather than captions under each cartoon frame. In July 1950, it changed its name to *The Dandy*.

The comic was full of cartoon strip characters whose fame endured for years. Korky the Cat, Keyhole Kate and Desperate Dan, for example, appeared in the first issue and all three were still going strong in the 1950s, when sales of the comic achieved two million a week.

It was not the kind of publication that would be expected to print science fiction. But, for two short series in 1956, *The Dandy* published an unusual double-page spread in each issue illustrated by one of their regular artists. His name was Eric Roberts.

Willie's Whizzer Broom

Roberts came from a London circus family and, after schooling, attended London's School of Art. In 1937, when *The Dandy Comic* was launched by D.C. Thompson, he joined the team as a freelance artist, drawing a cartoon strip called *Podge*. He also drew for *The Beano* and *Knockout*, as well as for several other short-lived titles that came and went after the Second World War.

In 1956, Roberts drew *Willie's Whizzer Broom* for *The Dandy*. The stories concerned a boy called Willie Meldrum who owned a magic broom, rather like the kind associated with witches, which he had found in his grandfather's joke shop. When he sat astride the broom and pressed a stud in the handle, it whisked him off to the year 2500.

The stories invariably involved Willie getting into trouble in the present, whisking himself off to 2500 to try to sort out his problem and immediately getting into even more trouble, very often with the future police. Nevertheless, he usually came across something unexpectedly that he could take back to the present to sometimes give him an advantage over the people or situation that had been his problem in the first place – but often landing him in even more trouble

The strip was originally drawn in black and white with a single spot colour, but later appeared in full colour.

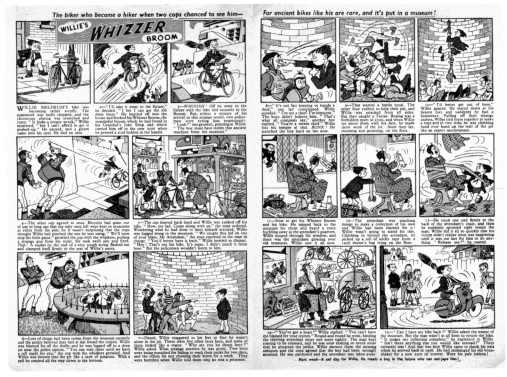

A *Willie's Whizzer Broom* adventure from a 1956 issue of *The Dandy*.

Daily newspaper strips

Comic strips of the 1950s didn't appear only in comics. They could sometimes be found in daily newspapers as well. The *Daily Express* had Jeff Hawke and the *Daily Mirror* featured Garth.

Jeff Hawke was the brainchild of Sydney Jordan, a Scottish aeronautical engineering graduate with a penchant for comic book art and science fiction. After assisting other comic strip artists for a while, he teamed up with two ex-RAF friends to create Jeff Hawke. Their hero was as an RAF pilot whose storylines ventured into the realms of science fiction.

The strip was bought by the *Daily Express* and appeared first in 1955. Unlike many other comic strip heroes, Hawke was more a diplomat than a fighter, and the three-frame comic strip that appeared each day in the newspaper nearly always featured weird and wonderful aliens. The aliens were usually more technically advanced than humans, rarely had violent tendencies and were often open to the diplomacy of Hawke and his friends.

Sydney Jordan, creator of the Jeff Hawke comic strip, photographed in 2016 at Lucca Collezionando, the Italian comics and games exhibition.

Unlike a lot of science fiction of the time, the strips were witty and amusing. Take, for example, this exchange between two aliens in one of the strips.

Alien one: 'Now that we are met in this fortuitous concurrence …'

Alien two: 'Can't you ever get down to brass tacks without all that cackle? Tell them bluntly we're the intergalactic police, and if they don't behave themselves, they'll be breakfast for the Bhorliks in one snap–crack of a snarg's snuffler!'

The strips were also somewhat prophetic in the way they touched on subjects such as the way humans were polluting their planet. Particularly prophetic was a strip published in 1959, in which a monument was seen commemorating the first human landing on the Moon on 4 August 1969. Ten years later, the actual moon landing happened on 20 July 1969, just two weeks earlier than the strip had predicted.

Publication ceased in 1974, by which time Jeff Hawke had become immensely popular not just in Britain, but also in Italy, Sweden and what was then Yugoslavia.

Garth was a very different character. The creator behind the hero was Frank Bellamy, a British comic strip artist best known for his work on *Eagle*.

Three strips from Sydney Jordan's *Jeff Hawke* series in the *Daily Express*.

The strip was first published in the *Daily Mirror* in 1943, ran through the 1950s and beyond, finally ceasing publication as late as 1997.

During his comic strip life, Garth developed super-human strength, which was a key aspect of his adventures. The plots were typical action-adventure stories, the science fiction twist being that they took part in widely spaced eras in time.

The hero of the *Daily Mirror* comic strips should not be confused with another Garth, also known as Aqualad and Tempest, a superhero who began life in DC Comics in 1960.

THE MAGAZINES

Science fiction in magazines goes way back to the Victorian era. At that time, many novels by well-known authors, prior to their publication in book form, were serialised in popular magazines of the day. They were usually written

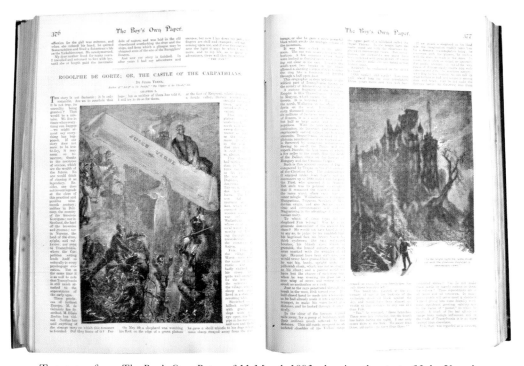

Two pages from *The Boy's Own Paper* of 11 March 1893, showing the start of Jules Verne's series.

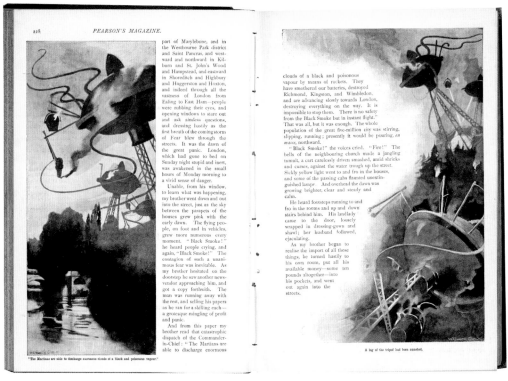

Two pages from an 1897 copy of *Pearson's Magazine*, part way through its serialisation of H.G. Wells's *The War of the Worlds*.

so that each episode ended with a cliffhanger that left readers wanting more and so encouraging them to buy the next issue to find out what happened next.

The March 1893 issue of *The Boy's Own Paper* – a weekly British magazine, priced one penny and full of stories, factual articles, jokes, puzzles and construction projects for teenage and younger boys – began a seventeen-part serial called *Rodolphe de Gortz, or The Castle Of The Carpathians*. It was an English translation of a story by French writer Jules Verne, already known for his science fiction novels.

The Castle of the Carpathians was a very early kind of science fiction cum horror story about strange happenings at a castle in the Carpathian Mountains of Transylvania where locals convince themselves the Devil is in residence. When a visitor to the region goes to investigate, he sees an image and hears the voice of a woman from his past who he had thought was dead.

Verne's story was published in book form when the serial ended in *The Boy's Own Paper*. It is sometimes suggested that the plot influenced Bram Stoker to write *Dracula*, which was published in 1897.

Pearson's Magazine was a monthly Victorian magazine for adult readers, containing mostly political and arts articles. It also published speculative fiction, and H.G. Wells was among its noteworthy contributors. In 1897, the magazine began the serialisation of Wells's *The War of the Worlds*, prior to its publication in book form in 1898. The serial was dramatically illustrated by Warwick Goble, a London-born artist who produced children's book illustrations and, when not drawing graphic pictures of Wells's Martian invasion, was known particularly for his pictures with Japanese and Indian themes.

It was, however, inventor, publisher, writer and editor Hugo Gernsback who is usually credited with being the man who published the first true science fiction magazine in 1923. It was called *Science and Invention*, and it was devoted to what Gernsback called scientific fiction. In 1924 he attempted and failed to launch a magazine called *Scientifiction*. But in 1926, he published

Hugo Gernsback, watching a very early television broadcast in 1928 when he was editor of the American magazine *Radio News*.

Just some of the great many science fiction magazines published in the 1950s, with others that continued their traditions throughout the following decades and beyond.

Amazing Stories, the first magazine devoted entirely to the genre. The years that followed were turbulent for the title, as it was passed from publisher to publisher, with a whole raft of editors, throughout the 1950s and onwards until it finally closed in 2005.

Like *Amazing*, most science fiction magazines of the 1950s originated in America, but there were companies who specialised in signing up British readers for annual subscriptions. The Atlas Publishing and Distribution company in London's East End advertised: 'Any scientific or technical magazine can be posted to you direct from the USA.' The average subscription charge in 1952 was around thirty shillings (£1.50).

Under an arrangement with their American publishers, some magazines were reprinted and distributed in Britain, where they sold for pre-decimal shillings and pence, rather than cents. There were also a small number of homegrown British magazines that copied the American style with garish and often lurid covers falsely representing less sensational stories inside.

Magazines sold in both countries conformed to two approximate sizes: octavo and the smaller digest. The latter was the more popular in the 1950s. The octavo magazines were apt to go for lurid covers; the digest magazines usually featured more tasteful and imaginative covers

One way that British readers could get their hands on American magazines in the 1950s.

with pictures connected to the stories within. What follows is just a small representation of personal favourites.

The Magazine of Fantasy and Science Fiction

To get the measure of how important *F&SF*, as the magazine was – and still is – affectionately known, you need only glance at the list of authors who contributed to the issue for December 1959. They included Ray Bradbury,

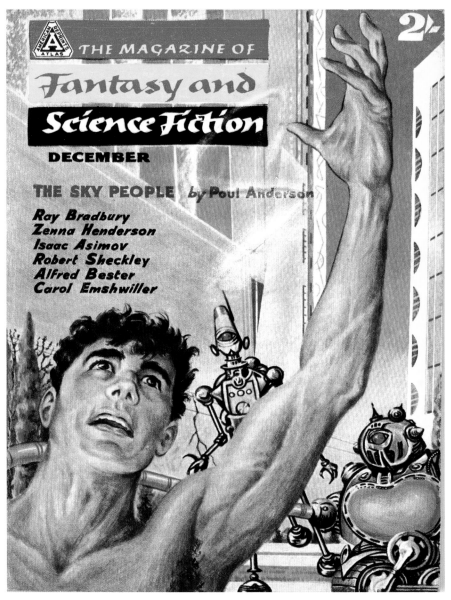

The British edition of a 1959 issue of *The Magazine of Fantasy and Science Fiction.*

Zenna Henderson, Isaac Asimov, Robert Sheckley, Alfred Bester and Carol Emshwiller – all eminent names known for the quality of their work and still to go on to even greater things in the years ahead.

F&SF was one of the big three American science fiction digest-size magazines of the 1950s – the other two were *Astounding Science Fiction* and *Galaxy Science Fiction*. It was first published as a quarterly magazine in 1949, became bimonthly in 1951 and monthly in 1952.

From the start, the magazine moved away from the sensationalism of the pulp magazines and set out to publish quality stories that rivalled those in the better-respected publications known in America as the slicks. It sometimes serialised novels, but was more concerned with short stories, covering a broad spectrum of styles and science fiction genres from a great many of the era's top authors.

The Magazine of Fantasy and Science Fiction is still published today.

Astounding Science-Fiction

Astounding was first published as a pulp size magazine in December 1929 with a cover date of January 1930. Its original title was *Astounding Stories of Super-Science*, but that was soon abbreviated to *Astounding Stories*. In early 1933 it went out of business, but resumed publication under a new publisher later that year. By the 1950s, after several incarnations, it had become a digest size publication.

The style of the magazine was for a harder kind of science fiction with plots that centred on action and adventure. It published many now legendary stories by top name authors, most notably Isaac Asimov's *Robot* and *Foundation* series and serials.

John W. Campbell Junior, the magazine's editor during the 1950s, was well known in the science fiction world for encouraging and shaping new authors, many of whom went on to greater things. In the years ahead, numerous stories first published in *Astounding* were collected into anthologies or turned into full-length novels.

By the end of the 1950s, with the approaching age of space exploration firmly set, it was decided that the magazine's title was no longer relevant to the new era. In October 1960, the name was changed to *Analog Science Fiction and Fact*, under which name it is still published today.

The British edition of a 1957 issue of *Astounding Science Fiction*.

No. 43

35¢

Price in Great Britain 2/-

The British edition of a 1953 issue of *Galaxy Science Fiction*.

Galaxy Science Fiction

The third of the big three American science fiction digest-size magazines, *Galaxy*, was first published in 1950 and was an immediate success, due in some part to the way its stories differed from those in its two main rivals. A typical story in *Galaxy* reflected the tastes of its founder and first editor, Canadian author H.L. Gold, whose interest lay in sociology, psychology and satirical humour.

Initially, it was undecided whether to call the magazine *Galaxy* or *If*. Mock-ups of both titles were produced and shown to writers, artists and fans, who voted for *Galaxy*.

The magazine attracted top authors of the day. Ray Bradbury's short story *The Fireman*, published in *Galaxy* in 1951, went on to be developed into the author's big selling novel *Fahrenheit 451*. Other luminaries such as Isaac Asimov, Robert Heinlein, Damon Knight, Clifford D. Simack and more were regulars in its pages. The magazine also spawned a series of books under the imprint of Galaxy Science Fiction Novels.

If was published as a separate magazine in 1952 and enjoyed moderate success. The magazine merged with *Galaxy* in 1974. Publication ceased in 1980.

New Worlds

Possibly the most influential British science fiction magazine, *New Worlds*, began life in 1946, having grown from a fanzine, launched a decade before and called *Novae Terrae*. The editor was John Carnell, who set the style for the magazine. Sales of the first issue were poor and Carnell blamed weak cover artwork. For the second issue he drew inspiration from American magazines of the time, commissioned a new style of cover and issue two sold out. Unfortunately, after the third issue, the publisher went bankrupt. Undeterred, Carnell raised £600 in capital to form a new company called Nova Publications with *Triffids* author John Wyndham as chairman. The first issue, under its new management, appeared in the spring of 1950.

The magazine's early years were successful but precarious. Then, in 1954, Nova Publications was acquired by a larger publisher, which gave it the stability to become a leading magazine in Britain.

J.G. Ballard, who would later go on to fame as the author of such books as *High-Rise*, *The Drowned World* and *Empire of the Sun*, made his first sale to *New Worlds*, thanks in part to the way Carnell recognised the importance of the author's style of writing.

John Brunner, whose book *Stand on Zanzibar* would later win the coveted Hugo, a prestigious literary award for science fiction writing, and who became one of Britain's most successful science fiction writers, was a regular contributor. Arthur C. Clarke, who at that time wrote mainly for the American market, also contributed. John Wyndham produced a series about a space-going family called the Troons, who later went on to star in his book *The Outward Urge*.

New Worlds ceased publication in 1970, but the name lived on in the titles of anthologies and various one-off publications.

Science Fantasy

In 1950, with the success of *New Worlds* established, the same publisher, Nova Publications, additionally produced *Science Fantasy* magazine. The editor was journalist Walter Gillings, who had been editor of another British magazine, *Tales of Wonder*, back in 1937. The first issue contained work by well-known authors of the era, including Arthur C. Clarke, with a story called *Time's Arrow*, about a time trip back to the days of the dinosaurs. The magazine also contained book reviews and non-fiction scientific articles.

Gillings lasted for only two issues as editor, when *New Worlds* editor John Carnell took over. Seeking to differentiate between the two magazines, he made a point of using only true science fiction in *New Worlds*, while adding more fantasy stories to *Science Fantasy*.

The magazine ceased publication in 1964, but was taken over by a new publisher and appeared again in 1966, first under the title *Impulse* and then *SF Impulse*. It finally closed in 1967.

The British edition of a 1954 issue of *Science Fantasy*.

Nebula Science Fiction

Nebula was a British magazine. It was launched in 1952 and held the distinction of being the only magazine of its type to be published in Scotland. It was launched and subsequently edited by teenager Peter Hamilton, whose parents ran a printing business in Glasgow. At the age of eighteen, Hamilton persuaded his father to use idle time on his printing press to produce, first a couple of science faction novels, and then a bimonthly magazine, although the true regularity of its appearance relied on when the company's printing press lay idle. The regularity also relied on how fast Hamilton could make money from one issue before starting production on the next. As it grew in popularity, however, and as printing was shifted to Dublin in 1955, publication became more regular.

Although lacking the input of some of those top writers who helped the American magazines flourish, *Nebula* still managed to pull in already established and soon-to-be-famous British writers who included Brian Aldis, Eric Frank Russell and Bob Shaw. It also helped that Hamilton tried his best to equal, and in some cases beat, the fees paid to writers by his rivals. American authors soon followed the British onto the pages of *Nebula*, with stories whose styles and plots were wide-ranging and seldom predictable. Early issues each contained a novella plus a few short stories. Later issues dropped the novellas to concentrate more on short stories.

By late 1957, the circulation was reported to be 40,000 and in January 1958 the magazine went monthly. Only around 25 per cent of its sales were in Britain, however. The other 75 per cent sold in America, Australia and, to a smaller extent, South Africa.

Unfortunately, towards the end of the 1950s, South Africa and Australia began to put limits on what could be imported into their countries. British excise duties didn't help either. Neither did the failing health of Peter Hamilton. The magazine went into debt and ceased publication in 1959.

Vargo Statten Science Fiction Magazine

Vargo Statten was one of many pseudonyms, used by British science fiction author John Russell Fearn. He was also a prolific writer of westerns and detective stories and one of the first British authors to appear in American pulp magazines. In a career that produced a torrent of novels and short

A 1954 issue of the *Vargo Statten Science Fiction Magazine*, one of the few home-grown British publications.

stories, he also wrote under the names Thornton Ayre, Polton Cross, Geoffrey Armstrong, John Cotton, Dennis Clive, Ephriam Winiki, Astron Del Martia, Hugo Blayne, Spike Gordon, Volsted Gridban, Paul Lorraine, Laurence F. Rose, Conrad G. Holt and quite possibly more.

Under the Vargo Statten name he wrote science fiction paperback novels for London publishers Scion Press, who then used the popularity of their author's name to launch a science fiction magazine in 1954. Statten was named as editor, but most of the editorial work was carried out by Associate Editor Alistair Patterson, with stories from several of Fearn's many aliases appearing prominently in the pages of each issue.

As well as science fiction stories from other popular authors of the day, the magazine featured letters from readers, book reviews, general editorial comments and even reviews of science fiction writers' stories published in rival magazines. An example of the kind of non-fiction commentary that kept readers abreast of what was going on in the science fiction world can be seen in this short gem published in the February 1954 edition.

Facetious Note: During the Christmas season there was a moment of great excitement at London Airport. Over the loudspeaker system a sepulchral voice announced: 'Hullo Earth, this is Rocket Ship *Luna* calling from outer space.' The airport officials failed to trace the ghost voice, but their matter of fact theory was that some reveller had managed to get access to an unguarded microphone. Rocket Ship *Luna* is the name of the space ship in the BBC's *Journey Into Space* serial. A mundane dénouement – at least it saved alerting the Vargo Statten magazine staff in readiness for the scoop of the century.

As was the case with many science fiction magazines of the 1950s, Vargo Statten's publication went through troughs and peaks during the time of its publication. In 1954, Scion Press got into financial difficulties and, in payment of one debt, passed control of the magazine to its printer, Dragon Press. Paterson resigned; Fearn took his place, but removed his pseudonym from the title, renaming the publication *The British Science Fiction Magazine*.

Despite getting a few prestigious names into the magazine, circulation took a dive and it didn't help when Dragon Press insisted on halving the fees paid to authors. With low submission rates, the quality of the stories dropped, and Fearn was forced to print stories of his own that had been rejected elsewhere. To save more costs, the size of the magazine was reduced.

In 1956, there was a national printers' strike in Britain. It forced Dragon Press out of business and the magazine ceased publication in 1956.

The British edition of a 1952 issue of *Thrilling Wonder Stories*.

Thrilling Wonder Stories

When science fiction supremo Hugo Gernsback lost control of *Amazing Stories* magazine in 1929, due to his company, Experimenter Publishing, going bankrupt, he started a new company called Gernsback Publications. It wasn't long before he launched three new magazines: *Air Wonder Stories*, *Science Wonder Stories* and *Science Wonder Quarterly*. The next year, the first two were merged under the title *Wonder Stories*, and the third one was renamed *Wonder Stories Quarterly*.

The publications weren't as successful as Gernsback might have hoped and, in 1936, *Wonder Stories* was sold to Beacon Publications, which already had magazines in its stable with the word *Thrilling* in their titles – *Thrilling Detective* and *Thrilling Love Stories* were two examples. So it made sense to add the word to the company's new acquisition. The title *Thrilling Wonder Stories* was born and the magazine continued to be published for close to twenty years.

By the 1950s, the magazine was established as a respectable science fiction magazine that often published brief, full-length novels as well as short stories. Well-known authors of the day such A.E. van Vogt, James Blish and Jack Vance were regular contributors, and Ray Bradbury had his first solo-written short story published in the magazine's pages.

Thrilling Wonder Stories ceased publication in 1955. The old *Wonder Stories* name was revived for two short-lived issues in 1957 and 1963.

Super Science Stories

This was not one of the most successful magazines of its time, enjoying only two brief runs, from 1940 until 1943, and then with a change of cover design from 1949 to 1951. The first editor was Frederick Pohl, who was still a teenager when he took over the role, but who went on to great things: later as editor of *Galaxy Science Fiction* and *Worlds of If* magazines, as well as the well-respected author of many successful science fiction novels in the 1970s and 1980s, for which he won several prestigious literary awards. He died in 2013 at the age of ninety-three.

During his time at *Super Science Stories*, and despite his publisher allowing him only to pay low rates, Pohl managed to attract writers like Isaac Asimov and Robert Heinlein at a time when their careers were just starting. He also

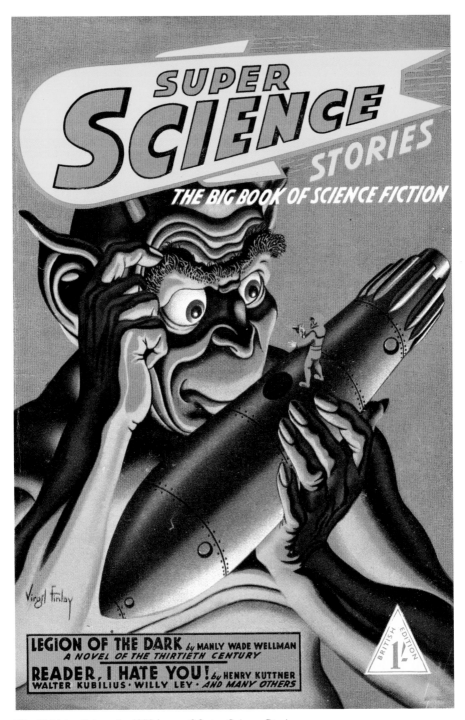

The British edition of a 1950 issue of *Super Science Stories*.

wrote many of the stories himself to fill space and to earn a little extra on top of the wage he was receiving as editor.

The magazine's first incarnation closed in 1943, but it was revived in 1949, just as the new golden age of science fiction was beginning. It continued to be published for nearly three years, closing in 1951.

A decade of magazines

The selected titles outlined above were among the better-known science fiction magazines of the 1950s, but they were by no means the only ones. During the decade of 1950 to 1959, there appeared a huge collection of magazines, mostly in America, fewer in Britain and around the English-speaking world. Some were published monthly, others bimonthly or quarterly. Many of them had begun life back in the 1940s, 1930s and even the late 1920s, and continued to be published into the 1950s. Others began life in the 1950s and continued into the years after. And there were those that began and ended their lives during the decade, some continuing publication for several years, others making only two or three issues before financial restrictions forced their closure.

As with much else in this book, which has been a personal rather than definitive trip through the science fiction world of the 1950s, the list that follows is not guaranteed to be complete. But it's as close as it can get to a list of all the amazing, fantastical, sometimes lurid, but always entertaining magazines that did so much to capture the very heart of the golden age of science fiction.

A. Merritt's Fantasy
Amazing Science Fiction
Amazing Stories
Analog Science Fact and Fiction
Astounding Science-Fiction
Astounding Stories
Authentic Science Fiction
Avon Fantasy Reader
Avon Science Fiction and Fantasy
   Reader

Avon Science Fiction Reader
Cosmos
Dream World
Dynamic Science Fiction
Famous Fantastic Mysteries
Fantastic
Fantastic Adventures
Fantastic Story Magazine
Fantastic Universe
Fantasy Book

British edition of *Future Science Fiction* that featured a story by John Wyndham, who found fame as the author of *The Day of the Triffids*.

Fantasy Fiction

Fantasy Magazine

Future Science Fiction

Galaxy Science Fiction

If

Imagination

Imaginative Tales

Impulse

Infinity Science Fiction

Nebula

New Worlds

Orbit Science Fiction

Other Worlds

Out of this World

Planet Stories

Rocket

Satellite

Saturn

Science Fantasy

Science Fiction Adventures

Science Fiction Digest

Science Fiction Plus

Science Fiction Stories

Science Stories

SF Magazine

Space Science Fiction Magazine

Space Stories

Space Travel

Spaceway

Superboy

Superman

Star SF

Startling Stories

Super Science Fiction

Ten Story Fantasy

The Magazine of Fantasy and
Science Fiction

Thrilling Wonder Stories

Tops in SF

Universe

Vanguard

Vargo Statten Science Fiction
Magazine

Venture Science Fiction Magazine

Vortex

Weird Tales

Worlds Beyond

Worlds of If

Picture Credits

Note on Illustrations

The author has made every effort to research the copyright status of all images included in this book, including contacting potential holders of copyright, either current or expired, to gain either their permission to reproduce an image or reassurance that an image is in the public domain. Any infringement of copyright as a result of their publication is entirely unintentional; if there have been any oversights, the publisher extends its apologies to the parties concerned and will update future editions of the book.

Cover picture: Derived from a poster for the 1956 film Forbidden Planet. Copyrighted by Loew's International. Artist(s) not known. Public domain, fia Wikimedia Commons.

Page vi: © John Wade.

Page viii: © The Atkinson, Southport.

Page ix: Courtesy of Catherine Warwick and Peter Hampson.

Page x: Courtesy of DC Comics.

Page xii: Television picture by Museokeskus Vapriikki via Wikimedia Commons.

Page xiv: Artwork by Bruce Gaffron, published with the permission of HarperCollins Publishers Ltd.

Page xv: Artwork by Ron Holloway.

Page 2: © John Wade.

Page 3: By Magnadyne Radio (progettista/costruttore) via Wikimedia Commons.

Page 5: By kind permission of the Hampstead and Highgate Express.

Page 6: Reproduced with kind permission of the Dan Dare Corporation Ltd.

Page 8: From the BBC Photo Library.

Page 10: By Bengt via Wikimedia Commons.

Page 15: Reproduced with permission of Pan Macmillan through PLSclear.

Page 93: Courtesy of www.freevintageposters.com. Originally distributed by Allied Artists.

Page 95: Courtesy of www.freevintageposters.com. Original © Universal-International.

Page 97: By Republic, public domain, via Wikimedia Commons.

Page 103: By Frank R. Paul, public domain, via Wikimedia Commons.

Page 104: Artwork by Bruce Gaffron. Printed with the permission of HarperCollins Publishers Ltd.

Page 105: Publicity picture, courtesy of *Writing Magazine*.

Page 107: Courtesy of Penguin Books.

Page 109: Courtesy of Penguin Books.

Page 111: Courtesy of Penguin Books.

Page 113: Courtesy of Penguin Books.

Page 115: Courtesy of Penguin Books.

Page 117: By Phillip Leonian from New York World-Telegram & Sun. Public domain, via Wikimedia Commons.

Page 119: Reprinted by permission of HarperCollins Publishers Ltd © 1960 Isaac Asimov.

Page 120: Reprinted by permission of HarperCollins Publishers Ltd © 1962 Isaac Asimov.

Page 122: Reprinted by permission of HarperCollins Publishers Ltd © 1964 Isaac Asimov.

Page 126: By Rob C. Croes / Anefo (Nationaal Archief), via Wikimedia Commons.

Page 127: Reproduced with permission of Pan Macmillan through PLSclear.

Page 130: Reproduced with permission of Pan Macmillan through PLSclear.

Page 132: Reproduced with permission of Pan Macmillan through PLSclear.

Page 134: Reproduced with permission of Pan Macmillan through PLSclear.

Page 136: Reproduced with permission of Pan Macmillan through PLSclear.

Page 137: By Alan Light via Wikimedia Commons.

Page 139: Originally published by Corgi, courtesy of Random House.

Page 141: Originally published by Corgi, courtesy of Random House.

Page 142: Printed with the permission of *The Magazine of Fantasy and Science Fiction*.

Page 144: Originally published by Corgi, courtesy of Random House.

Page 147: Reproduced with permission of Pan Macmillan through PLSclear.

Page 149: Courtesy of Penguin Books.

Index